Before it came, one of the soldiers recognized the danger. Calling out to his companions, he rose and turned to run. He wasn't fast enough. The blast rocked both vehicles, its shrapnel taking down the would-be runner like a point-blank shotgun blast. It also burst the lead jeep's fuel tank and ignited a spare can of gasoline on the rear deck of the passenger compartment, instantly enveloping both vehicles in flames.

Watching from cover, Bolan saw a handful of soldiers burst from cover, all of them on fire and beating at the flames with blistered hands. They ran instead of dropping to the ground and rolling, partly out of panic, and because the turf around them was on fire, as well. A lake of burning fuel surrounded them, allowing nowhere to go except a mad rush for the tree line that would offer no help, no shelter.

Bolan left them to it.

MACK BOLAN ®
The Executioner

The Don Pendleton's®
Executioner®

NUCLEAR REACTION

A GOLD EAGLE BOOK FROM
WORLDWIDE®

TORONTO • NEW YORK • LONDON
AMSTERDAM • PARIS • SYDNEY • HAMBURG
STOCKHOLM • ATHENS • TOKYO • MILAN
MADRID • WARSAW • BUDAPEST • AUCKLAND

For James Morton

First edition January 2007
ISBN-13: 978-0-373-64338-7
ISBN-10:   0-373-64338-1

Special thanks and acknowledgment to
Mike Newton for his contribution to this work.

NUCLEAR REACTION

Printed in U.S.A.

It is ironical that in an age when we have prided ourselves on our progress in the intelligent care and teaching of our children we have at the same time put them at the mercy of new and most terrible weapons of destruction.

—Pearl S. Buck, 1892–1973
What America Means to Me

Demagogues and terrorists have too many weapons in their arsenal. Somebody needs to draw a line, and this one's down to me.

—Mack Bolan

THE
MACK BOLAN
LEGEND

Nothing less than a war could have fashioned the destiny of the man called Mack Bolan. Bolan earned the Executioner title in the jungle hell of Vietnam.

But this soldier also wore another name—Sergeant Mercy. He was so tagged because of the compassion he showed to wounded comrades-in-arms and Vietnamese civilians.

Mack Bolan's second tour of duty ended prematurely when he was given emergency leave to return home and bury his family, victims of the Mob. Then he declared a one-man war against the Mafia.

He confronted the Families head-on from coast to coast, and soon a hope of victory began to appear. But Bolan had broken society's every rule. That same society started gunning for this elusive warrior—to no avail.

So Bolan was offered amnesty to work within the system against terrorism. This time, as an employee of Uncle Sam, Bolan became Colonel John Phoenix. With a command center at Stony Man Farm in Virginia, he and his new allies—Able Team and Phoenix Force—waged relentless war on a new adversary: the KGB.

But when his one true love, April Rose, died at the hands of the Soviet terror machine, Bolan severed all ties with Establishment authority.

Now, after a lengthy lone-wolf struggle and much soul-searching, the Executioner has agreed to enter an "arm's-length" alliance with his government once more, reserving the right to pursue personal missions in his Everlasting War.

Prologue

Darice Pahlavi wondered if this would be the last day of her life. She'd spoken of it with the others, when she'd offered to complete the task that no one else within their circle could perform. The rest were all sincere enough, but none of them had access to the data that was needed.

Only she was *inside*.

She recognized the irony. A generation earlier, no woman of her nationality or faith would have been educated adequately, much less trusted to participate in such events.

But things had changed. In that respect, at least.

Some things, she feared, would never change. The lust for power that consumed some individuals was as powerful as ever. The egomania that warped their view of life and everything around them, made them believe that only they were fit to make the life-or-death decisions that affected thousands, even millions.

Perhaps Pahlavi herself had shared a measure of that guilt, she thought. But she had woken up in time to save herself. To save her soul.

The question burning in her mind was whether she could save her nation, and perhaps the world at large, from a horrendous nightmare in the making.

It could mean death if she failed, but she felt compelled to try.

Concealing the material had not been difficult. The two computer CD-ROMs were slim enough to hide beneath her clothing. She had taped them to her inner thighs, which were slim enough that she did not produce a plastic scraping sound with every step she took. The tape was uncomfortable, but it would hold its grip.

She'd delayed the taping until she was nearly finished for the day. It would've been a dicey proposition, working all day in the lab, with two disks plastered to her thighs, but she could easily endure an hour of discomfort, walking to the bus outside and riding to her home. Once she was there, and safe from prying eyes…

She caught herself relaxing prematurely and cut short her reverie. She wasn't home yet, wasn't even close. A hundred things could still go wrong.

Anxiety overwhelmed her, made her wish that she could run back to the washroom, but she couldn't go again so soon. It might provoke an inquiry. Was something wrong? Was she unwell? Did she require examination by the lab's standby physician? Had she been contaminated in some way?

Once Dr. Mehran started asking questions, Pahlavi knew she'd be finished. It would mean a physical examination, which would instantly reveal the contraband beneath her skirt. The mere suggestion of an illness in the lab provoked decisive and immediate responses that were carved in stone, a law unto themselves.

If she appeared in any way unusual, Pahlavi would be doomed, as surely as if she *had* been fatally exposed to the materials they handled every day.

She pinched herself, a cruel twist of her flesh beneath the long sleeve of her lab coat. She had to remain focused. Any small distraction, any deviation from routine, might raise a red flag with security as she was leaving.

There was no innocent excuse for smuggling confidential data from the lab. Taking a box of paper clips was considered serious. Stealing the data at the very heart of their most secret program would be tantamount to suicide.

Pahlavi knew it wouldn't be a quick death, either. They would want to ask her questions, find out how and why she dared to take such risks. Who was she working for? Had she accomplices? Being a woman, she would not impress interrogators as a ringleader, much less an operative who conceived and executed such activities alone. If nothing else, theft of the disks signaled that she planned to pass them on, reveal their secrets to some third party, whether for ideology or profit.

She wasn't sure how long she could protect her brother and the rest, once the professionals began to work on her with chemicals or pure brute force. Her pain threshold had never been extraordinary, and fear had weakened her already, as if her own body was conspiring with her enemies.

Biting the inside of her cheek to make her brain focus on simple tasks, Pahlavi went through the same cleanup routine she had followed every day since starting at the lab. There was a place for everything, and everything had to wind up in its proper place before she could depart. Slovenly negligence invited criticism and a closer look from Dr. Mehran, which she definitely didn't want.

Her fellow lab workers were chatting as they cleared their stations, making small talk that she couldn't force her mind to follow. What did she care if a certain film was playing at the theater, or if a coworker's insipid cousin had been jilted by his third fiancée in as many years? She was on a mission vitally important to them all.

After hanging up her lab coat, she retrieved her bag and trailed the others from the lab, toward the security checkpoint where guards routinely opened briefcases and purses, pawing through their contents, but were otherwise content to let the workers pass. Darice couldn't recall the last time a lab employee had been frisked or asked to empty pockets.

It was with a sense of panic, then, that she beheld the guards in front of her this day. Two extra had been added to the team, a man and woman, both equipped with flat wands she recognized as handheld metal detectors.

Pahlavi was certain she would faint, but she recovered by sheer force of will. She couldn't pass inspection with the wands, which left two choices. Either she could double back and ditch the CD-ROMs, or she could find another way out of the lab complex.

Was there another way?

Determined to find out, she turned, making a show of searching through her purse as if for something she'd misplaced, and quickly walked back toward the lab.

Southwestern Pakistan

"The trick," they'd warned him, "isn't getting in or out of Pakistan. It's getting in *and* out." Eight hours on the ground, and Mack Bolan already had a fair idea of what they'd meant. He'd been here before.

Aside from its northwestern quadrant, ruled by Pashto-speaking clans who'd never paid a rupee to the government in taxes and who'd rather strip an unknown visitor down to his skin than offer him the time of day, the bulk of Pakistan was long accustomed to a thriving tourist trade. British adventurers had led the way, when Pakistan was still a part of India, and during modern times there'd never been a dearth of hikers, mountain climbers, or exotic hippie-types who came to groove on Eastern vibes and drugs.

The country welcomed everyone, but getting out could be a challenge. Departure meant an exit visa, often challenged by venal immigration officers at the eleventh hour, when they noticed various "irregularities" that triggered new and unexpected fees or fines. Export of anything resembling antiquities could land a tourist in hot water, as much as the drugs and weapons that were sold as freely in most market towns as fresh produce. Rugs purchased in Pakistan required an export permit, even when the local vendors ardently denied it and refused to furnish them.

Getting in was easy, getting out required finesse.

But at the moment, Bolan's main concern was how to stay alive while he completed his work in Pakistan.

The nation as a whole was dangerous, no doubt about it. Some observers ranked Karachi as the world's most hazardous city, with an average of eight political murders each day, compounded by the toll of mercenary street crime.

Shopping for hardware in Karachi had been easy, once the Executioner found the dealer recommended to him by his contacts at Stony Man Farm, in Virginia. Many Pakistani arms merchants, like the drug traffickers, would sell to foreigners, then rat them out to the police for a reward on top of what they'd already been paid. Bolan's contact, he'd been assured, was "straight." He'd sell to anyone and squeal on no one, understanding that his business depended on discretion as the better part of valor.

In the dealer's cramped back room, Bolan had surveyed the merchandise and had gone Russian for the rifle, picking out an AKMS with its folding metal stock, together with a dozen extra magazines. For antipersonnel grenades, he chose the reliable Russian RGD-5s. He'd gone Swiss for his side arm, choosing a SIG-Sauer P-226, the 9 mm with a 15-round magazine, its muzzle threaded to accept a sturdy sound suppressor. His final purchase was a fighting knife of uncertain ancestry, with a twelve-inch blade, serrated on the spine, and a brass pommel stud designed for cracking skulls. Once he'd put it all together in a duffel bag, he was good to go.

Go where?

He had directions and a detailed map, and a satellite phone

in case he absolutely needed immediate help in English. If that happened, Bolan reckoned it would be before he met his contact.

If he met his contact.

Negotiating the Pakistani countryside was at least as perilous as crossing a chaotic street in downtown Lahore or Karachi. Dacoits—well-organized bandits who often worked straight jobs by day, then moonlighted as highwaymen—posed one potential obstacle to travelers. And local warlords might exact tribute from passersby while drug runners or traffickers in other forms of contraband were prone to spilling blood whenever they encountered a potential witness to their criminal activities. Plus, a thriving black market revolving around kidnapping for ransom, all ensured the backcountry was dangerous indeed.

But so was Bolan.

His potential adversaries simply didn't know it yet.

The Executioner kept a keen eye out for bandits and for government patrols as he drove north from Karachi toward Bela. He was supposed to meet his contact, maybe plural, at a rest stop west of Bela, and he didn't want police or soldiers stopping him along the way, perhaps searching his Land Rover and asking why he needed military weapons for a drive around the countryside. The less contact he had with men in uniform, the better for his mission.

Bela was nothing much to look at, once a visitor got past the gaudy marketplace, and Bolan had no need to stop or browse. He headed west from town, and fifteen minutes later saw the rest stop on his right, two hundred yards ahead, precisely where it had been indicated on his map.

Slowing, he pulled into the graveled space and parked beside an old four-door sedan with several shades of primer paint laid on, in something very like a camouflage design. The car was empty, and he sat behind the Rover's wheel, letting the engine idle while he waited for his contact to appear.

A creak of rusty springs, immediately followed by a scrape of leather soles on gravel from his left rear told Bolan that he'd been suckered. He was half turned toward the sound when he heard someone cock a pistol. Turning more, he could see the weapon pointed at his face, held by a young man with solemn eyes.

The gunman frowned and said, "The weather is not good for travel."

"But a soldier has no choice," Bolan replied.

Still cautious, the gunman dropped the muzzle of his Beretta 92 toward the ground and used the decocking lever to release its hammer harmlessly. He did not slip the pistol back into his belt, however. He shifted it to his left hand as he advanced toward the Land Rover, holding out his empty right.

Having correctly answered with the password for their meeting, Bolan stepped from his vehicle, eye flicking toward the old sedan, its trunk ajar. Two more armed men stood watching him. They'd risen from their hiding place on the old car's floorboards.

"It was hot, I guess, inside that trunk," Bolan said.

His handshake indicated strength, the gunman thought. "Hot," he granted, swiping at his sweaty forehead with the back of his right hand. "How was your journey from Karachi?"

"Uneventful," Bolan replied. "The way I like it." Nodding toward the two other men, he inquired, "Are they with you?"

"They are," the contact said. "In these times, we take no unnecessary risks."

"Unnecessary risk is never wise," Bolan said. "You want to trust me with a name?"

There seemed no point in lying, and he'd never used an alias, in any case. "Pahlavi. Darius Pahlavi. Yours?"

"Matt Cooper. Are we talking business here?" Bolan asked.

"I think not. It would be unfortunate if a patrol should come along."

"Where, then?"

"In the hills nearby," Pahlavi said. "I have a safe place there."

The Executioner considered it, but only briefly. Making up his mind, he said, "All right. You ride with me and navigate. Give us a chance to break the ice."

Pahlavi didn't hesitate, despite his natural misgivings. This American had traveled halfway around the world to meet him and assist his cause, if such a thing was even possible. Pahlavi knew that he had to draw the line between caution and paranoia at some point.

"Of course," he said, then turned and gave instructions to the others in Urdu, telling them to follow closely and be ready if the stranger should betray them. Neither one looked happy with Pahlavi's choice, but they did not protest.

As Pahlavi climbed into the Land Rover, he considered the risk he'd taken—communicating with the United States, when Washington supported the regime in power, mildly cautioning its leaders on their worst excesses while refraining from decisive action to control them.

It had been a gamble, certainly, but once Pahlavi passed on what he knew, via a native said to be a contract agent for the CIA, the answer had been swift in coming. The Americans would send someone—a single man, they said—to see if he could help Pahlavi.

Not to kill his enemies, per se, or see them brought to ruin, but to see if he could *help*.

Whatever that might mean.

As they pulled out, Pahlavi glanced behind the driver's seat and saw a duffel bag, zipped shut. He couldn't tell what was inside it, but he had already glimpsed the slight bulge underneath the man's windbreaker, which told him the American was armed.

And why not, in this land where human life was cheaper than a goat's? Only a fool would face the unknown in the living hell his homeland had become, without a weapon close at hand.

Above all else, Pahlavi hoped that the American was not a fool. Intelligence and skill were more important than his personality—although it wouldn't hurt if he dispensed with the persistent arrogance Americans displayed so often in their dealings with "Third World" nations.

What he needed was a man to listen and to *act*.

But what could any one man do, that Pahlavi and his allies had not tried themselves? he wondered.

"Have you a plan?" he asked, embarrassed by his own impatience, even as he spoke.

"I need to know the details of your problem, first," Bolan replied. "My briefing on the other side was pretty…general, let's say."

"Of course." Pahlavi nodded. "I apologize. You see, my sister—"

The Executioner had already seen the military vehicles approaching from the opposite direction. He could hardly miss the driver of the lead vehicle slowing to stare at them, while one of his companions leaned in from the back seat, mouthing orders that he couldn't hear.

"That's trouble," Bolan said, as they rolled past the two jeeps and the open truck behind them, filled with riflemen in uniform.

"It is," Pahlavi agreed, turning in his seat to track the small convoy. He was in time to see the lead jeep make a U-turn in the middle of the two-lane highway, doubling back to follow them.

"I make it six or eight to one," Bolan remarked. "Smart money says we run."

"Agreed."

Bolan floored the accelerator, surging forward with a snarl from underneath the Land Rover's hood. "All right," he said. "This is the part where you're supposed to navigate."

2

Lieutenant Sachi Chandaka was often bored on daylight patrol. Encounters with bandits were rare, since the scum did their best to avoid meeting troops or police, and the most he usually expected from an outing in the countryside was some sparse evidence of crimes committed overnight by persons he would never glimpse, much less identify or capture. He supposed some criminals transacted business when the sun was high and scorching hot, but most of them dressed in expensive suits and had plush offices, where they sipped coffee and decided the fate of peasants like himself.

The fact that he was often bored did not mean the lieutenant's wits had atrophied, however. On the contrary, his eyes were keen and he could *feel* malice radiating from an undesirable at thirty paces. More than once, while working in plain clothes or killing time off duty, he had startled his companions by selecting sneak thieves from a market crowd, all ordinary-looking men, then watched and waited while the petty predators moved in to make their snatch.

Perhaps it was a gift. Chandaka couldn't say and didn't really care, as long as he could work that magic when he needed it the most.

From half a mile away, he'd seen the two vehicles standing

at the rest stop, on the south side of the highway. At a quarter mile, he'd counted four men idling by the cars, presumably engrossed in conversation. By the time his small convoy rolled past, the men were back in their cars, two passengers in each. Even someone as dull-witted as his driver, Sergeant Lahti, had to have known that they were criminals.

It wasn't so much what the four men did, as what they didn't do. It was unnatural for anyone surrounded by vast tracts of nothingness to keep his eyes averted as a military convoy rumbled past, almost within arm's reach. And yet, among the four men in the two vehicles, only the driver of the lead car even glanced across the pavement at Chandaka's jeep.

One man—and he was not Pakistani.

European, possibly. Perhaps Australian or American. In any case, Chandaka meant to find out who the four men were, what business brought them to the highway rest stop outside Bela in the middle of the afternoon, and why three of them were determined not to let him see their eyes.

"Turn back!" he snapped at Lahti. "Follow them!"

"Follow?" The concept didn't seem to register.

"Yes, Lahti. Turn the steering wheel. Reverse direction. *Follow them!*"

"Yes, sir!"

Once Lahti understood an order, he would do as he was told. It would not cross his mind to question a superior. Lahti had found his niche in life, performing simple tasks by rote, relieved that someone else was always close at hand to tell him what came next.

Chandaka braced a hand against the jeep's dashboard, as Lahti powered through a sharp U-turn. He saw the startled visage of the corporal who drove the second jeep in line. Chandaka pointed after the westbound vehicles, and shouted, "Follow them!"

There was no time to clarify the order. Lahti stood on the accelerator. Something rattled loosely, underneath the jeep's drab hood, then power surged and they started gaining ground on the retreating vehicles.

Chandaka wished he had a rifleman beside him, but if it came to shooting on the highway, he would simply have to do the job himself. He had a Spanish CETME Model 58 assault rifle propped upright in the narrow space between his knees, butt on the floorboard, and now he hefted it, getting its feel.

He'd never shot a man before, or even shot *at* one, but training made the difference. When the time came, if it came, Chandaka knew that he would be prepared and would perform as his superiors expected. He was not afraid. Indeed, the feeling he experienced was closer to elation.

At long last, it appeared something was happening.

Lahti was bearing down, gaining ground, but the lieutenant felt obliged to chide him for the sake of feeling in control, being a part of it. "Don't let them get away," he ordered.

"No, sir!"

If Lahti took offense, it didn't show.

The two cars were within one hundred yards, and the gap was narrowing. The army jeeps weren't much to look at, but they had surprising power. No auto manufactured in the country could outrun them, and among the foreign imports, only certain sports cars or a Mercedes-Benz would leave them in the dust.

If that began to happen, Chandaka was prepared to win the race another way. He gripped his rifle tightly, drew the bolt back and released it, chambering a round. He did not set the safety.

They were already too close for that.

"Faster!" he urged, leaning forward in his seat, straining at the shoulder harness.

"Yes, sir!" the sergeant replied.

Sixty yards. Soon, Chandaka would be able to make out the license number of the second car. At that point, he'd decided he would radio headquarters and report himself in hot pursuit—something he should've done already if he had been going strictly by the book. Someone's secretary could then begin to trace the license and find out who the rabbits were, or more likely come back with the news that he was following a stolen car.

"Get up there, Lahti, so that I can read the license plate!"

"Yes, sir!"

Lahti leaned forward, as if it would help them gain more speed. Chandaka almost smiled at that, but it was frozen on his face as someone in the car ahead of them began firing a submachine gun through its broad rear window, spraying bullets toward Chandaka's jeep.

THE BLAST OF AUTOMATIC fire surprised Adi Lusila, nearly made him swerve the car into a roadside ditch. One moment, he was concentrating on the highway and Pahlavi in the car ahead of him, trying his best to leave the soldiers in his wake, and then Sanjiv Dushkriti blew the damned back window out, turning the car's interior into a roaring wind tunnel.

Lusila shouted at Dushkriti. "What possessed you?"

"A great desire to stay alive," Dushkriti answered, then craned back across his seat to fire another short burst from his L-2 A-3 Sterling submachine gun. One hot cartridge stung Lusila's ear, then fell into his lap.

"Take care with that!"

"It's no good from here," Dushkriti said, by way of an apology, and turned to scramble awkwardly between their seats, climbing into the back. One of his boots glanced off the gearshift as he made the move. Lusila cursed at the grating sound it made.

The grating sound was followed by a loud clang.

"We're hit," Dushkriti said, and sounded almost pleased about it. "Do not worry, Adi."

Idiot, Lusila thought. They were pursued by soldiers, with a foreign stranger driving Darius ahead of them, and now Dushkriti had provoked a running battle that would likely get them killed.

"Don't worry?" Lusila said with a sneer.

A sudden laugh surprised him, coming out of nowhere and erupting from his throat. He was hysterical. It was the only diagnosis that made any sense at all. If he pulled over now, right where he was, perhaps there was a chance that he could plead insanity. Laugh all the way to jail and through his trial, praying to land in an asylum, rather than a basement torture cell or execution chamber.

Not a chance, Lusila thought.

The soldiers were already shooting at him, thanks to Dushkriti. Even if he stopped and raised his hands, with an armed madman in the car they wouldn't grant him any time for pleas or explanations.

He would simply have to run, and when escape was clearly an impossibility, beyond the palest shadow of a doubt, then he would have to fight.

And die, of course.

What other outcome could there be when four men stood against some thirty-five or forty?

And it might not even be four men, Lusila realized. Pahlavi and the tall American might keep on going if he stopped to fight. They could use the distraction to escape and save themselves.

To carry on the mission.

Adi Lusila flinched from that idea, as if it were a stinging slap across his face. Pahlavi wouldn't ask for such a sacrifice. He would give up his own life first, to save his friends. But losing him was not in the best interest of their cause.

A bitter taste had wormed its way onto Lusila's tongue, matching the stench of cordite in his nostrils. In between the bursts from Dushkriti's Sterling, he could hear return fire from the jeep behind them, now and then a bullet slamming home into his vehicle.

"Hang on!" he warned, and began to swerve across the two-lane highway, back and forth, hoping his serpentine progress would make it harder for the soldiers in the jeep to kill him, likewise spoiling any shot they might've had at Pahlavi and the American up front.

"My stomach!" Dushkriti cried.

"Are you hit?"

"Car sick!"

"So, puke and keep on firing!"

When a new stink filled the car, Lusila gave thanks that the rear window was gone. Let the foul odors from his friend blow back along the highway toward their enemies and sicken them, instead.

Dushkriti finished gagging, rattled off another burst of automatic fire, then growled, "I need another magazine."

He hunched down in the back seat, fumbling in his jacket pocket, thereby giving Lusila his first clear view of their pursuers since the chase began in earnest. Even as he glimpsed the lead jeep in his rearview mirror, the officer in its front passenger seat shouldered his rifle, aimed and fired as Lusila swerved the car again.

He nearly outsmarted himself, turning *into* the shot, rather than away from it. The bullet whistled past Dushkriti's head and clipped a corner of the rearview mirror, then punched through the windshield with a solid crack. Lusila cursed and started swerving more erratically, letting his fear dictate his moves as much as logic.

"Stop!" Dushkriti shouted. "I can't load the gun!"

"Try harder, then!" Lusila snapped. "They almost took my head off!"

With a sharp metallic clacking sound, Dushkriti mated his magazine with the Sterling's receiver, then cocked it once more and pushed up on his elbows, preparing to fire.

It was a fluke, Lusila thought, the soldier in the jeep behind them choosing just that moment to unleash another shot. What were the odds of it? Much less that he would somehow manage to anticipate Lusila's movement of the steering wheel.

It was a miracle of sorts that the next bullet drilled Dushkriti's forehead and exploded through his shaggy hair in back, spraying a gray-and-crimson mist across Lusila and the dashboard gauges.

It was his turn, then, to fight the rising tide of nausea and pray that he could keep his old car on the road while bullets hammered at it from behind.

"WHAT'S HAPPENING?" Pahlavi asked, half turning in his seat.

Bolan glanced at the rearview mirror, then came back to focus on the long, straight two-lane road. "They're under fire," he answered. "Taking hits."

"But fighting back, yes?"

"From the sound of it. You want to tell me where we're going?"

"Five more miles," Pahlavi said. "There is a road into the hills. It leads to my safe place."

"It won't be safe for long if we lead soldiers to the doorstep," Bolan told him. "What's Plan B?"

"Plan B?"

"Your backup. Something else on tap, when things go wrong."

Pahlavi's stricken face told Bolan there was no Plan B. "I did not think there would be soldiers here," the Pakistani said. "They almost never pass this way in daylight."

"'Almost' obviously doesn't cut it," Bolan said.

"I'm sorry. Let me think."

"Think fast!"

More firing erupted from behind them, and the second car was definitely taking hits from one rifle, maybe a couple of them. In his mirror, Bolan saw a bullet chip the windshield from inside, before the driver started swerving like a drunkard. He guessed it was the best the other man could think of, while his partner laid down cover fire but couldn't seem to score a solid hit.

"There are some woods ahead," Pahlavi blurted out. "Perhaps three miles. If we can lead them there, perhaps—"

"It's worth a shot," Bolan said, even as he thought about the killer odds. He'd counted twenty-four men in the open truck, plus two inside the cab, two in the lead jeep, four more in the second, which meant they were outnumbered eight to one.

Those weren't the worst odds he had ever faced, granted, but Bolan didn't know how skilled his companions were at combat. If the one's wild shooting with the submachine gun was any indication, they might be more liability than help in a firefight.

A tiny splash of color in his rearview mirror drew the warrior's eye, in time to see the second car in their high-speed procession swerving more erratically than ever. Bolan couldn't tell who'd been hit, the shooter or the driver, but he worked it out a second later, when the car stayed on the road and didn't stall.

One down, he thought, judging from all the blood. And since the driver couldn't likely fight off thirty hostile troops while racing down the two-lane blacktop, Bolan guessed that he would soon be number two with a bullet.

"Adi and Sanjiv!" Pahlavi moaned. "We must stop for them!"

"Get real," Bolan said.

"We must!"

"Did you drive out here just to die?" Bolan asked. "I had the impression there was something you've been trying to accomplish."

"But my friends—"

Pahlavi turned again and looked down the road in time to see the second car whip through a fair bootlegger's turn, using a technique requiring fair coordination of the brake and the accelerator, which when executed properly reversed the direction of a vehicle 180 degrees in a fraction of the time required to make a U-turn.

"What's he doing?" Pahlavi asked.

"Buying us some time," the Executioner said with approval.

Having reversed himself, Lusila accelerated once again toward the short convoy pursuing him. He had his right arm out the window, blazing at the soldiers with a pistol while he closed the gap between them, taking heavy hits along the way.

Bolan supposed Pahlavi's comrade might've rammed the lead jeep—if he'd lived that long. Instead, the rifle bullets found him when his charger and the jeep were still some twenty yards apart. Maybe his foot slipped off the clutch and let the engine stall, or maybe other rounds had ripped in through the grille and hood. In any case, his vehicle veered off the pavement, coasting to a smoky halt with its blunt nose and front tires in a ditch.

"We're on our own," Bolan advised Pahlavi. "How much farther to those woods?"

"Not far," Pahlavi said, speaking as if he had something caught inside his throat.

"I hope you're right. "Either way," the Executioner informed him, "we'll be running out of time within the next few minutes."

"We can fight them, yes?" Pahlavi asked. "For Adi and Sanjiv!"

"They're done," Bolan reminded his grief-stricken passenger. "Try fighting for yourself."

"Of course. We must survive to finish what we've started."

"Right," Bolan replied. "And maybe if we do, you'll tell me what that is."

"Fight first, talk later," Pahlavi said. "Yes?"

"I've heard that song before."

Flicking his eyes between the highway and his rearview mirror, Bolan searched the roadside for a hint of woods. An endless ninety seconds later, he saw shadows on the roadside ahead, and recognized them as a mass of trees.

One smallish forest, coming up.

And thirty-two trained riflemen to make it one more patch of Hell on Earth.

3

The first round from the lead jeep's shooter ricocheted from Bolan's trunk and chipped the frame of his rear window prior to hurtling off through space. Instead of weaving crazily across the road, he poured on all the speed he had to offer, hunching lower in his seat to give the rifleman a smaller target.

Beside him, Darius Pahlavi had regained enough control to draw his pistol, swivel in his seat and return fire from his side window. It was awkward, but at least it let him shoot right-handed without smashing out their back window.

Bolan supposed incoming rounds would do that soon enough, unless he reached the woods before the soldiers on his tail improved their aim.

He had a quarter mile to go, and then he had to hope there was some kind of access road into the forest, or he'd wind up parking on the berm and leaping from the car in full view of the soldiers who were primed to kill him. Bolan hoped Pahlavi had more sense than that, but their acquaintance was too brief for him to judge the man's state of mind.

Rattled was one term that immediately came to mind, but now that he was fighting back, Pahlavi seemed to have a better grip, reaching inside himself somewhere to find his nerve.

After his third shot, Bolan's passenger gave out a whoop of

triumph. Bolan checked the rearview mirror and made out a spiderweb of cracks covering half of the jeep's windshield. It hadn't stopped them, but it slowed the soldiers a little. They fell back to blast at Bolan's car from a position out of pistol range.

It gave Bolan the edge he needed, while his enemies were putting on their brakes, maybe a little shaky in their haste and from the shock of a near-miss. He took advantage of it, burning up the road and gaining back some of the ground he'd lost in the pursuit. It was two hundred yards or so until they reached the first trees, and he was looking for a turnoff, any place where he could leave the two-lane blacktop for a while.

"There, on your left!" Pahlavi urged him, pointing, and the road appeared almost by magic, cut for the convenience of emerging eastbound traffic, but still good enough for Bolan's exit, heading west.

"Hang on!" he said, and swung the steering wheel to make it, rocking with the vehicle as the tires complained, then found their grip again and powered over gravel, onto rutted, hard-packed soil.

The road would be muddy, miserable in the rainy season, but the day was bright and dry. Bolan hung on as they shuddered along the washboard surface, barely one lane wide. It was too much to hope the army truck might find the road impassable, but maybe its progress would be retarded. Let it fall behind the jeeps a bit, spread out the hunting party, and it might work out to Bolan's benefit.

"They're after us!" Pahlavi warned.

"That's no surprise. Is there another turnoff anywhere ahead?"

"Half a mile, I think. The road begins to circle back, but there's a branch off to the left."

Even alert, Bolan almost missed it, braking at the last instant and swerving hard into a narrow access road that cut off to the south-southwest. The surface was rougher, punished by the elements for years without repair or even simple maintenance. Still, Bolan held his steady speed as best he could, praying the shock absorbers and the ball joints wouldn't fail him.

After roughly a hundred yards, they reached a clearing in the woods, with room enough for five or six pup tents around a campfire. Bolan used the space to turn, tires spitting dirt and gravel, until he was facing the direction of the access road. He killed the engine and sat a moment, listening to the hot metal ticking as it cooled.

"What are you doing?" Pahlavi asked with a nervous tremor in his voice.

"No way they missed our turnoff," Bolan said. "No way we can get past them, going back the way we came. That only leaves one option." He was reaching for the duffel bag behind him as he spoke. "We fight."

"So many of them?"

"That, or let them take you down."

Pahlavi didn't have to think about it. "No," he said.

"Then I suggest you get out of the car and find some cover while you can."

Matching his words to action, Bolan stepped out of the vehicle, taking the keys, and started running hard in the direction of the tree line, thirty feet away.

SACHI CHANDAKA WORRIED that he might be following his prey into a trap. It seemed bizarre that bandits would deliberately sacrifice two men, but if he thought about it in another way, it *did* seem possible that he had stumbled on some small conspiracy, put them to flight, and only now would they attempt to kill him with an ambush.

This was bandit territory, beyond any doubt. Why shouldn't one gang or another have a stronghold somewhere in the woods around him. Maybe those he was pursuing had a cell phone or a two-way radio, allowing them to call ahead to set the trap.

"Slow down a bit," he ordered Lahti. "Keep the car in sight, but don't be hasty."

"Yes, sir."

Chandaka couldn't tell if Lahti was relieved or not, and he did not particularly care. Glancing behind him, the lieutenant saw the second jeep and open truck behind it keeping pace, jerking with every rut and pothole in the miserable unpaved road. There would be aching bladders in the truck, he guessed, but they would have to wait.

Ahead, he saw the car they were pursuing leave the main track, veering left onto another narrow road, its surface even rougher than the one they traveled. Chandaka held his rifle, finger on the trigger, peering through the windshield veined with cracks that radiated from a central bullet hole.

"Sir, shall I follow them?" his driver asked.

"Of course, but cautiously."

"Yes, sir."

Lahti slowed a little more, the vehicles behind them doing likewise. By the time they cleared the turn, Chandaka couldn't see their quarry anymore. He nearly panicked, fearing he had lost the bastards after all this effort and would have to back out of the woods, exposed to hidden riflemen on every side.

"Hurry!" he ordered, contradicting his original instruction. "Find them!"

"Yes, sir." No enthusiasm whatsoever sounded in the sergeant's voice.

They jounced along the narrow track, tree branches almost meeting overhead, casting the roadway into shadows that seemed sinister under the present circumstances. Lahti kept his eyes fixed on the road ahead, leaving Chandaka to watch out for snipers, booby traps, and any other rude surprises that their enemies might have in store for them.

The clearing took Chandaka by surprise. One moment, they were running through a narrow corridor of trees, the next, they nosed into an open space some sixty feet across, walled in by forest on all sides. He saw the bandit car ahead, its grille aimed toward his jeep, but with the doors open and no one left inside. Which had to mean—

"Look out!" he barked at Lahti. "Stop!"

Lahti slammed on the brakes, heedless of the vehicles behind him, and Chandaka fancied he could hear a short cry of alarm from Corporal Dekhar in the second jeep before it struck the rear of his vehicle with impressive force. A lance of pain tore through Chandaka's neck and shoulder blades, but he had no time to consider it, as gunfire crackled from the tree line.

"Ambush!" he called out to no one in particular. A glance at Lahti told him that the sergeant couldn't hear him. He slumped sideways against his shoulder harness, dark blood spilling from a bullet hole above one eye.

Cursing his pain, Chandaka threw himself out of the jeep, clutching the CETME rifle to his chest. He hit the ground running, gunfire ringing in his ears, as bullets filled the air around him.

He had no idea how many bandits were unloading at him from the forest, but his own men were returning fire in awkward fashion, spraying bullets here and there in lieu of finding clear-cut targets. It was a wasted effort, but Chandaka couldn't blame them. They were panicking, taken completely by surprise.

And it was all his fault.

Chandaka stopped, crouching, and sought a target of his

own. Where were the bastards? Had they cut him off? Was it too late to slip away?

The thought shamed him. Chandaka held his weapon in a tight, white-knuckled grip and started edging back in the direction of the jeeps and truck. They were his only cover, short of plunging right into the trees, and that was clearly hostile territory.

He would rally his command, devise a strategy, and make the bandits sorry they had ever crossed his path, or he would die in the attempt.

And at the moment, Chandaka knew it could still go either way.

BOLAN SQUEEZED OFF a burst from his AKMS and watched one of the soldiers topple screaming from the open truck. He hadn't planned on waging war against the native military quite this soon, but he was in it now, and there was nothing left to do except his best, fighting to stay alive.

He'd lost track of Pahlavi when they separated, no time to coordinate their action, but he hoped the young man would be circumspect, fire only when he had a target, and conserve his ammunition for the shots that he could make. Perhaps he could retrieve another weapon from the field, if he ran out of ammunition for his pistol, but whatever happened, he was on his own.

Bolan kept moving, stopping long enough to fire a short burst from the shadows, constantly in motion when he wasn't lining up a shot. The duffel bag was slung across his shoulder, riding heavily against his left hip as he moved, but short of pocketing its contents Bolan couldn't let it go. He needed the spare magazines, the frag grenades, to help him shave the odds against these unexpected adversaries.

He was halfway through a 30-round box magazine and had

reduced his distance from the truck by forty feet or so, when he decided it was time to give his enemies another shock. Palming one of the RGD-5s, he pulled the pin, mentally counted down from six seconds to four, then lobbed the green egg toward the jeeps where they sat nose-to-tail, with gunners crouched behind them.

No one saw the grenade coming, not until it landed on the broad hood of the second jeep with a resounding clang and wobbled for a heartbeat, as if making up its mind which way to go. The RGD-5 wasn't round, and so its path was unpredictable. It bounced, then slipped into the small space left between the two jeeps, where the second one had rammed into the first.

Bolan hunched down and waited for the blast. Before it came, one of the soldiers recognized the danger. Calling out to his companions, he rose and turned to run. He wasn't fast enough. The blast rocked both vehicles, its shrapnel taking down the would-be runner like a point-blank shotgun blast. It also burst the lead jeep's fuel tank and ignited a spare can of gasoline on the rear deck of the passenger compartment, instantly enveloping both vehicles in flames.

Watching from cover, Bolan saw a handful of soldiers burst from cover, all of them on fire and beating at the flames with blistered hands. They ran instead of dropping to the ground and rolling, partly out of panic, and because the turf around them was on fire, as well. A lake of burning fuel surrounded them, allowing nowhere to go except a mad rush for the tree line that would offer no help, no shelter.

Bolan left them to it, ready with his automatic rifle as the other troops began to reassess their situation. Knowing they were all at risk, the soldiers redoubled the outpouring of their aimless fire into the forest, bullets flaying bark from tree trunks, clipping branches, ventilating leaves.

Bolan was relatively safe from being spotted, in those circumstances, but a stray round through the head or chest was just as deadly as a sniper's well-aimed killing shot. He stayed low, took advantage of the cover, firing only when he had a target dead to rights and in the clear.

Where was Pahlavi? he wondered.

Never mind.

Survival was the first priority. If he could deal with the remaining soldiers and emerge alive, there would be time enough to look for his elusive contact. In the meantime, it was strictly do-or-die.

The jeeps were destroyed, but the Executioner heard the truck's big engine cranking, as someone tried to get it started after stalling it.

Bolan rose and sighted on the cab. The soldiers surrounding it were firing wildly. His angle wasn't optimal, he had no real view of the man in the driver's seat, but he was lined up on the left-hand door. Taking a chance, he held the autorifle's trigger down and used the last rounds in his magazine to ventilate that door, spraying the inside of the cab with sudden death.

The engine fell silent, and the troops around the truck's cab scattered, seeking better shelter from the storm that had enveloped them. Reloading in a rush, Bolan moved on.

4

Darius Pahlavi was no longer terrified. Somehow, somewhere between the death of his two friends and his arrival in the forest clearing with Matt Cooper, he had passed from numbing fear to a sensation that he barely recognized.

Rage was a part of it, for all he'd lost and all his people had endured—the nightmare that they *would* endure, if he failed to complete his mission. There was guilt, as well, for leading Adi and Sanjiv into the trap that claimed their lives. He vowed to make amends with Adi's wife and Sanjiv's parents somehow, someday.

If he lived that long.

Right now, he had to focus on surviving for the next few minutes, which meant ducking bullets in the woods and doing everything he could to stop his enemies.

Kill them, Pahlavi silently corrected himself. It all came down to that. Kill or be killed.

He'd never shot a man before that afternoon—never shot at a man, in fact—and when it happened, the sheer deceptive ease of it surprised Pahlavi. He had practiced with the pistol earlier, knew how to aim and squeeze the trigger slowly, without jerking it, but mortal combat put a different slant on things.

His first shots, on the highway, had been wasted but for one that cracked the windshield of the jeep behind them. Too late, even then, to save his friends, but he'd felt a rush of satisfaction from the simple act of striking back.

It was a different thing, of course, to fire at living men on foot, instead of faceless autos on the highway, but it helped that these men were intent on killing him, had killed his friends already.

Cooper had taken down a number of the enemy already, firing with an automatic rifle, then contriving somehow to destroy their jeeps. Pahlavi found it horrible and fascinating, all at once, as if he had been dropped into the middle of some action film from Hollywood.

Except that there were real bullets whining around him, thunking into trees raising spouts of sod on impact with the ground. Real bullets, too, inside his pistol, waiting to be used against his foes.

Pahlavi found a vantage point where he could watch the soldiers. Several of them were hunkered down behind their truck, waiting for orders or an opportunity to move. Cooper had pinned them down, but he was somewhere on the other side. These troops apparently had no idea there was another enemy watching, on *their* side of the truck.

Pahlavi took his time, aiming, worried a bit that he was letting Cooper down by not advancing more aggressively. But he knew he would do the tall American no good at all if he was dead. Aiming, he framed a target in his sights as he'd been taught—but then the soldier moved, shifting away, duckwalking toward the rear of the truck. Cursing, Pahlavi tracked him, had him lined up when the soldier rose and stepped around the tailgate, rifle at his shoulder, squeezing off a burst toward the far side of the clearing.

Pahlavi squeezed the trigger, rode the sleek Beretta's recoil, hopeful but still surprised to see his target crumple, back arched, slumping to the earth. The soldier writhed, convulsing, kicking at the sod, then shivered out and moved no more.

Pahlavi had expected nausea, a rush of guilt, *something* besides the mere sense of a job well done, but nothing came to him. Perhaps it was the moment, he decided, too much going on around him to permit normal emotions coming to the fore.

Or else, perhaps he *liked* it.

No. Pahlavi wouldn't, couldn't think about that now. There would be ample time to psychoanalyze himself if he survived this battle and the mission still to come.

And if he died, what difference would it make?

Soldiers were grouped around the man he'd shot, checking for vital signs. Some of them were firing aimlessly into the woods. They clearly had no sense of where the fatal shot had come from, meaning he could fire again, at least once more, with relative impunity.

Pahlavi chose another target, lined his sights up on the soldier's chest, and let the hammer drop.

SACHI CHANDAKA HUDDLED underneath the truck and tried to understand exactly what was happening. He'd been pursuing four men, with a force of thirty-one behind him, and he'd seen two of them die. The others should be dead by now, as well, but instead *his* men were dying all around him, while he cowered in the shadows, trembling and in pain.

He had been splashed with burning fuel, along one sleeve and shoulder of his jacket, when the jeeps exploded moments earlier. Ducking and running to escape the shrapnel and clear the spreading lake of fire behind him, the lieutenant had been pulled down by two privates who smothered the flames and doubtless saved his life. Chandaka reckoned they should both receive citations for their courage and quick thinking, but from where he lay beneath the truck, he saw one of them stretched out dead, almost within arm's reach.

His pain and fear immobilized Chandaka, shamed him. He knew he should find the strength to rally his remaining troops, lead them to victory, and thus salvage some shred of honor from this day—but how?

At present, he had no idea how many enemies were firing at his soldiers from the forest, whether they were bandits or guerrillas, why they'd sought this confrontation. It was preposterous to think that he had simply stumbled onto them, and any hint that he was only dealing with the two men they had chased into the woods seemed like insanity.

Two men alone could never do all this.

Could they?

But even if there were a dozen shooters in the woods, Chandaka still had them outnumbered. Even with his losses, he could still attack—use "shock and awe," as the Americans were fond of saying. He should storm the tree line with guns blazing and destroy the bastards who had bloodied and humiliated him.

In fact, there was no other choice. He could not simply lay beneath the truck and wait until his men had all been killed, then wriggle out to face the enemy alone. Nor could he wait and pray for reinforcements to arrive, since none of his superiors knew where he was, or even that he was in trouble.

Right, then, he told himself. He had to act, and swiftly, to redeem the situation and himself.

Groaning, Chandaka dragged himself from underneath the truck, pulling his rifle after him. Some of his soldiers seemed surprised to see him, as if they'd forgotten he was with them, or perhaps assumed that he'd been killed. They huddled under fire, some of them hammering long bursts into the tree line closest to them, seemingly without a hope of scoring any hits.

Chandaka started counting heads, got to fourteen and realized that there were no more left to count. He couldn't do the simple calculation in his head, so rattled was he by the evidence before his eyes, but the lieutenant understood that more than half his soldiers had been lost.

All dead? Had some of them turned tail and run? he wondered.

It made no difference now. He'd have to work with what he had.

Feigning a confidence he didn't feel, Chandaka told his men, "We cannot stay here. They'll murder all of us unless we seize the—"

"Who are they?" someone demanded, interrupting him.

"It doesn't matter," the lieutenant answered. "We must now seize the initiative. Carry the fight to them. I need you all to follow me and—"

Something dropped out of the sky and landed at Chandaka's feet. He glanced down at it, blinking. It seemed ludicrous—a bright green apple or a ball, some kind of toy— but one of his men shouted, "Grenade!" and they began to scatter in a panic.

Whimpering, Chandaka turned to run. He managed two long strides before the antipersonnel grenade exploded. Its concussion plucked him off his feet and punched him through an airborne somersault, while shrapnel tore into his body with the lancing pain of countless razor blades. Chandaka landed on his back, rolled over once and wound up staring at a smoky sky.

Survival was beyond him now. He knew it. It had been too much to hope for. Chasing bandits and guerrillas was a game for better men. He'd failed the army and his soldiers and himself, but none of that seemed relevant. Instead, he focused on the pain and hoped that it would end soon.

There was only so much that a man could bear.

BOLAN WAS READY WHEN the soldiers broke from cover, sprinting to escape the frag grenade. His AKMS had a fully loaded magazine, and even though the weapon's fire-selector switch didn't allow for 3-round bursts, Bolan was deft enough to manage on his own.

He led the first runner by three feet, give or take, and stroked the rifle's trigger lightly, sending three or four 7.62 mm rounds downrange to meet him, take him down and keep him there.

The second man heard firing away to his left and returned it without even looking to see where it had come from, still running, but blasting away with his weapon in hopes of distracting the sniper who'd just nailed his friend. With luck, it might've worked, but this one's luck had run out.

Bolan squeezed off another burst and saw his target stumble, drop his rifle, throwing out both arms as if to catch himself, but they were limp before he hit thc turf facedown and plowed it with his chin, doing a spastic little break-dance in the dirt before he died.

How many left?

Bolan could see five runners, guessed there had to be several others out of sight, beyond the truck, but he would have to take them as they came.

Incredibly, two of the soldiers were advancing toward his position at a dead run, high-stepping across uneven ground and making decent speed. He didn't know if they had spotted him, or if they'd picked a point at random as their destination, but it made no difference.

He shot the nearer of the runners first, a quick burst to the chest that slammed him over backward, head and shoulders touching down before his heels made contact with the earth. That snapped the second soldier out of any trance that may have gripped him, and he started firing from the hip, still charging, mouthing challenges or curses in a language Bolan couldn't understand.

Bullets were whipping over Bolan's head when he tattooed the soldier's chest with four rounds on the fly and spun him, autorifle still blazing away, through a pirouette. His legs started to buckle halfway through it, folding so that he appeared to screw himself into the ground.

Turning on his mark, Bolan lined up another target as the man glanced toward the source of gunfire, making eye contact. He was about to squeeze the rifle's trigger when another shot rang out, somewhere ahead and to his left. It was a pistol, and the bullet caught his man in midstride, dropping him with an expression of immense surprise upon his face.

Pahlavi?

Bolan didn't have the time to ponder it, with two soldiers still moving in his field of fire. The farthest from him was about to reach the tree line, all of sixty feet away, but that was nothing for the AKMS in a marksman's hands. The rifle stuttered briefly, blasting spouts of blood from olive drab fatigues, and Bolan saw his man go down, sliding a few feet on his belly, arms outflung, before his head butted against a tree and stopped him short.

The last soldier Bolan could see was running for his life, his knees and elbows pumping, with the rifle in his fists clearly forgotten. Even with the echoes of the battle ringing in his ears, Bolan could hear the soldier panting, straining toward the finish line that offered momentary safety.

He could let the runner go, grant him the gift of life, but

that would jeopardize the mission, Darius Pahlavi and himself. It was a risk Bolan was not prepared to take, this early in a brand-new game.

He fired and caught his target on the fly, a puff of crimson rising from the soldier's head and shoulder as he tumbled, rolling over once, then shuddering a moment on the grass before his life ran out and left him hollow, still.

There could be others waiting for him on the far side of the truck, but Bolan had to take that chance. He didn't want to waste another grenade on corpses, without checking first to see if there was any threat. That meant emerging from the trees with caution, making his advance one slow step at a time.

Halfway around the truck, the Executioner saw Pahlavi standing at the tree line opposite, exposed to any soldiers still alive behind the truck. No one was firing at him, which encouraged Bolan to advance more quickly. As he cleared the truck's tailgate, he found that his second grenade had done its work effectively, if not cleanly. There were no more hostile survivors on the field.

Pahlavi wore a slightly dazed expression as he crossed the grass to stand at Bolan's side. "All dead?" he asked.

"It looks that way," Bolan replied.

"Now, what?"

"Now," Bolan said, "we move this truck and see if we can get my rental out of here before the cavalry shows up. And while we're on the road, we need to talk."

5

Southwestern Pakistan

The open highway wasn't safe, but it was all they had. They couldn't fly, and even as they passed through wooded areas, Bolan knew they could not afford to hide and hope the storm would pass them by.

He didn't spend much time watching network news broadcasts, but Bolan knew that a loss of thirty-odd soldiers in one firefight would rock Pakistan. Some would mourn the loss, others might cheer it, but the powers that be would most certainly seek to explain and avenge it.

This would be no minor gale. They were fleeing ahead of a full-fledged tornado, the kind of storm that could pluck them off the face of planet Earth and never let them go. The kind that could make them evaporate without a trace.

They have to find us first, Bolan thought.

After he had put two miles between them and the slaughter site, he asked Pahlavi, "So, where are we going?"

"To my village. It's the only place we will be relatively safe."

That "relatively" wasn't very reassuring, but the Executioner would take what he could get, just now.

"How far?" he asked.

"About one hundred miles, due north," Pahlavi answered.

Bolan checked his fuel gauge. They should make it with a bit of gas to spare, if there were no detours along the way, but any traveling beyond their destination would require a fill-up.

"Right," he said. "Then we've got time to talk. You start, and take it from the top."

"The top?"

"From the beginning," Bolan translated.

"Of course. My sister is…she was a nuclear physicist. She made an honor and distinction for my family, not only graduating from the university, but second in her class. The government immediately offered her a post with their new laboratory, working on a program they call Project Future. It's supposed to harness nuclear power for peaceful applications. Generation of electric power and the like. I don't pretend to understand it all."

"And then your sister—that's Darice?" Bolan asked, reflecting on the meager intelligence he'd been given.

"It was." A sadness there. Clearly, Pahlavi reckoned she was dead.

"And then Darice found something else," Bolan suggested.

"Yes! She soon discovered that there was a plan *within* a plan, involving Sikh extremists. Project X. While some employees at the lab worked on the project everybody knows about, others were put to work behind the scenes, trying to build a compact weapon that would fit inside a piece of luggage. Darice was assigned to that division, banned from talking to the scientists working on Project Future. Banned from talking, period."

"But she still talked to you," Bolan suggested.

"Yes. We have been close since childhood, Mr. Cooper. Closer still, since we lost our parents seven years ago. Their bus collided with a train, and…"

Staring out his window into space, Pahlavi briefly lost his train of thought, then came back to it, waving off the lapse without comment.

"In any case," he said, "she told me what was happening. Together, we decided something must be done to stop it, either halt production on the small bomb or prevent it being passed to other hands. You know the history of Pakistan and India?"

"I've just had a refresher course," Bolan replied.

"Our leaders hate each other. I'm not sure they still remember how or why it started, but the hating has become a way of life for both countries. It's unhealthy, but I don't know how to change it. If it even *can* be changed. Our countries fight like children over lines drawn on a map, who claims this bit of land or that, as if the soil itself is somehow precious. Kashmir, for example, is a situation I will never understand."

"How's that?" Bolan asked.

Pahlavi shrugged. "Eighty percent of all the people living there are Muslim, like myself and my government, but it is ruled by Hindu leaders. It reminds me of South Africa, the white and black, or Protestant and Catholic in Belfast. Yes?"

Clearly, Darice Pahlavi hadn't been the only member of her family to get an education. It was Bolan's turn to shrug. "It happens. If we're lucky, governments can work it out."

"But these two only fight and threaten. Never really talking, never listening. For this, they've gone to war three times in forty years, but nothing is resolved. Why either country wants more mouths to feed remains a mystery to me."

"So, that's the rub," Bolan said. "And you're thinking there may be another war."

"If Pakistan supplies a suitcase bomb to Sikh extremists and they use it against India?" Pahlavi's smile was bitter as he shook his head. "The next war will destroy life as we know it here, and possibly throughout the world. There are alliances, support agreements. If one nation uses its atomic bombs against the other—"

Pahlavi shook his head again, slump-shouldered. At a glance, it seemed that he had aged ten years while he was talking, in the time it took Bolan to drive five miles.

"Let us assume," Pahlavi said, "that the retaliations are confined to the subcontinent. Nearly two billion people live here. That's about one-fourth of the whole planet's population. Even if the fallout never drifts beyond our borders—an impossibility, all scientists agree—most of those people will be lost, either in bombings of the cities or through radiation poisoning, starvation and disease. Beyond that, if the fallout spreads…"

"I get it," Bolan said.

"And don't forget the various alliances, treaties and nonaggression pacts. Who knows what's written down somewhere and hidden in some diplomatic vault? Will the Chinese move in? The Russians? Either way, it means reaction from the U.S.A. and Britain, probably the UN, too. Picture the world on fire."

Bolan had been there in his head, a thousand times. He didn't like the view.

"What was your plan, at first?" he asked.

"Darice would smuggle out proof of Project X, for distribution to the media. Once the conspiracy was public knowledge, those responsible would either have to stop or face the condemnation of a world united to oppose them."

"But she never made it out," Bolan observed.

Pahlavi's eyes were misty now. "I still don't know what happened, how they found her out. I've been in hiding since the day she…disappeared. The government wants me and everyone involved in our group, Ohm, to silence us. Even the politicians who might once have raised their voices against Project X show a united face against a threat to national security."

"So," Bolan asked him, "what's your alternative plan?"

Pahlavi was quiet.

"What's your alternative to going public in the media? You can't do that without the evidence, so what's up next? Why am I here?" Bolan asked.

Pahlavi swallowed hard. "We have no other choice," he said. "We must destroy the roots of Project X."

Although the thought had not been far from Pahlavi's mind since the loss of his sister, it still intimidated him to speak the words aloud.

"All right," Bolan said. "Spell it out. What have you got in mind?"

"Perhaps to penetrate the laboratory somehow," Pahlavi replied. "Once inside, there should be some way to destroy the weapon and its plans."

"Perhaps? Somehow? Some way?" Bolan glanced over at him, then back toward the road. "That's not a plan. It's wishful thinking."

Embarrassed by the truth of the American's words, Pahlavi said, "I grant you that I do not have full knowledge of the laboratory, how to get inside, or what to do there. I was counting on Darice to help us. She…we talked about the lab, of course. Security precautions, all the measures they employ to keep strangers out. I know where the lab is located, the best way to approach it, but I'm not a soldier. Until recently, I never thought that I would have to be."

"Sometimes it sneaks up on you," Bolan said. "But once you come to the decision, there's no turning back."

"I understand."

"Do you?"

"I know that it may mean my death," Pahlavi said.

"But not just yours. How has the rest of Ohm been taking this?"

"You saw Adi and Sanjiv die for us. The others feel the same."

Bolan frowned. "Can you be sure of that?" he asked.

Pahlavi felt his hackles rising. "Ask me what you mean to say."

"It's SOP—standard operating procedure—for a government to infiltrate opposing groups whenever possible, keep track of what they're planning." Bolan spared another quick glance from the two-lane highway. "It may be an absolute coincidence that a patrol with thirty-odd soldiers came along just at the time we were supposed to meet, but then again, maybe it *wasn't*."

"You believe there is a traitor in the group?" Pahlavi asked.

"I don't believe or disbelieve," Bolan replied. "I'm saying it's a possibility you should consider, if it hasn't crossed your mind already."

"You're wrong," Pahlavi answered stubbornly. "Darice and I joined Ohm. They did not come to us with flattery, pretending to believe as we did. As I do."

"All the more reason to consider who your friends are," Bolan said. "The group has been around a while. Presumably it's known to the security police, maybe G-2."

"I do not understand."

"Army Intelligence," Bolan explained. "I don't know what you call it here. I guarantee your government has one or more departments dedicated to collecting information on its opposition, doing everything it can to bring them down."

"Of course." Pahlavi thought about it for a moment, suddenly uneasy. "But if what you say is true, then we are doomed."

"Not necessarily," Bolan replied. "First thing, remember that I'm only saying *if*. What *if* there was a mole inside. Then he or she may not know where we'd go, in case the setup fell apart. Be careful who you trust, is all I'm saying."

"But you ask me to trust you," Pahlavi said in challenge.

"The difference is that *you* called *me,* and I'm from the outside. You've also seen me stand against your enemies. A double agent wouldn't do that. Couldn't risk it."

To that logic, there was no response. Pahlavi knew that the American was correct. No traitor working inside Ohm would kill soldiers to keep his cover story solid. His superiors surely would punish such an act with death, perhaps the execution of the man's whole family.

Or woman's, Pahlavi thought, riven with suspicion. His mind had moved along those lines before, of course, but each time he'd found some excuse to tell himself it was impossible. No traitors could exist within the group he'd come to trust with everything—his life, his sister and his sanity.

Pahlavi would have cursed Cooper for raising all those ugly doubts again, but the American was simply speaking honestly, forcing Pahlavi to confront a possibility that he had been remiss in overlooking previously.

"Now, I'll ask again," Bolan said. "What's our destination?"

"Still my village," Pahlavi said. "It is not Ohm that we run to, but the people I grew up with. If they betray me, then it's better that I simply die."

"Your call on that," Bolan remarked. "But if it's not too much to ask, try not to take me with you, okay?"

"You need not fear my people, Mr. Cooper."

That brought no response from the American, but it suddenly occurred to Pahlavi that if the people of his village failed him, *they* might have something to fear from the

American. He had already seen the man in action, killing all but three or four of the soldiers who had been slain that afternoon.

It hit Pahlavi full force that he was not the same man he had been that morning. In the meantime, he had killed and watched friends die. He was a fugitive now, from whatever passed for justice in his homeland. The authorities could not stop heroin from passing through the country on its way to Europe, and they might be scheming to ignite another war with India for no good reason, but they would be out in force to find him, because of this day's bloody work.

And now, he might be bringing sudden death into the very village where he had been born and raised.

But where else could he go?

Nowhere.

"You have nothing to fear," Pahlavi said again. And hoped that it was true.

"Another thing you need to think about," Bolan remarked. "We don't know when they'll find the bodies, but it may not be too long. For all we know, they may have sent out bulletins while they were chasing us, before we led them off the road. If they know how to run a search, they'll work out from the killing ground and won't give up until they find something. If you're already on a list, and they know where you came from, well…"

He left the statement dangling, let Pahlavi finish it himself. There was another risk to which he would expose his people, but he still had no alternative. If he could not run back to Ohm, which had no central headquarters in any case, then only in his native village could he hope for sanctuary.

"We will not stay long," Pahlavi said. A compromise. "Just long enough to get supplies, and then…"

Pahlavi hesitated. He was fresh out of ideas. It shamed and angered him that he could not present a finished plan to the American. But if he'd known exactly what to do and could complete the mission on his own, the American would not be there.

"Let's try a different angle of attack," Bolan said. "Tell me what you know about the lab and Project X."

6

"Explain to me what happened," Cyrus Shabou said. "I wish to understand how such a thing occurs."

A grim-faced man in full-dress military uniform sat opposite the deputy minister for defense, separated from Shabou by the wide teak plateau of his handmade desk. The gleaming emblems on his collar marked him as a colonel. He was, in fact, Anish Dalal, commander of all counterterrorism actions in the western third of Pakistan. And clearly, he did not enjoy a summons from the civilians who controlled the very life or death of his career.

"Deputy Minster," Dalal began, "I am unable to supply as full an explanation as you might expect, and as I would prefer to give. From all appearances, Lieutenant Sachi Chandaka was leading a routine patrol when he encountered someone on the highway west of Bela."

"Someone?" Shabou interrupted. "He encountered *someone?*"

"If I may continue, sir?"

"By all means, do so. And explain yourself."

"At 1420—that would be—"

"I know the military clock, Colonel. Proceed."

"Yes, sir. At 1420, Lieutenant Chandaka broadcast a brief message, reporting himself in pursuit of two unidentified vehicles, each with two or more male occupants. They were reportedly proceeding northward, but there were no further bulletins. At 1900, Lieutenant Chandaka's patrol was officially late, without word of progress or location. Radio queries went unanswered. We finally received a call from a police outpost in Balochistan. They'd located a civilian vehicle with two dead men inside and evidence of gunfire. We launched a local search immediately and we found the rest."

Shabou frowned and tapped a manicured index finger on the printout set before him, on his desktop. "Thirty-two men dead, including the lieutenant, and three military vehicles destroyed. Is that correct?"

"Essentially," Dalal replied. "The truck was not destroyed, as I'm given to understand the term, but it was damaged. Yes, sir."

"And you still have no idea at all who may have been responsible for this?"

"Sir, we've begun with the assumption that the dead civilians on the highway are related to the massacre."

"That seems a logical conclusion, Colonel," Shabou replied.

"Yes, sir. Both were armed, of course. Their weapons had been fired, but further tests will be required to tell if any of their bullets actually struck Chandaka's vehicles. In any case, their car was found roughly three miles away from where the others died."

"Have you identified these two?"

"We have, sir. Their names were Sanjiv Dushkriti and Adi Lusila. Both in their twenties, the first born in Karachi, the other in Hyderabad. Dushkriti served six months as a student for hashish possession. Lusila was clean. They were driving his car. Nothing else in the vehicle, besides their weapons, to suggest a criminal intent."

"And what of politics?"

"They're not on file, Deputy Minister. There were no manifestos in the vehicle. No drugs or extra weapons, as if they were trafficking. My guess would be that they were highway bandits, interrupted by the sight of a patrol. They run, Chandaka chases them, and there's a fight."

"A *fight?* Is that how you describe the loss of thirty-two trained men, with only two dead on the other side?"

"Perhaps my choice of words—"

"I would describe it as a massacre," Shabou pressed him. "Do you agree?"

"In retrospect…yes, sir."

"And is it common for a pair of highwaymen to massacre so many soldiers, then escape unharmed?"

"Sir, you'll recall they lost two men."

"In the initial fight, three miles or more from where our soldiers died."

"Yes, sir."

"How many bandit dead were found among our men?"

"None, sir."

"In which case—"

"But they sometimes carry off their dead and wounded, sir," Dalal said.

"Now you presume a larger group of bandits? Where did they come from? Where did they go? How were they able to appear at will and take advantage of a chance encounter on the highway?"

"Sir, we have no answers to those questions yet. You understand, of course, that our investigation is still in the preliminary stage."

"In that case, I suggest that you accelerate, Colonel Dalal— or I may find someone with more initiative and energy to take your place. I hope we understand each other," Shabou said.

"Yes, sir. Absolutely."

"Good. I won't detain you any longer, since you still have work to do and supervise."

Dalal rose stiffly to attention, waiting for Shabou to return his textbook salute, then turned on one heel and marched out of the office. Shabou waited another moment, then called out, "He's gone. You can come out now."

A side door opened to admit Kurush Gazsi. Impeccable in linen, each and every one of his retreating hairs in place, Gazsi crossed swiftly to the chair Dalal had vacated and sat before the desk.

"You heard him," Shabou said, not asking.

"Yes."

"What did you think?"

"Perhaps the officer in charge of the patrol was an incompetent. Perhaps he was decoyed into a trap."

"I hear too much 'perhaps,' these days. I need answers, solutions. Can you help me?" Shabou asked angrily.

"Not with highwaymen," Gazsi replied. "But I can check the names of the dead gunmen against known members of Ohm. If there's a match, we may be onto something."

"What, exactly?" Shabou asked.

"Again, sir, without the connection, I cannot be sure. But Ohm was damaged by our interception of their spy. I have no doubt that they will seek revenge at some point. They might even try to raid the lab if all else fails."

"What of the woman's brother?"

"Still at large," Gazsi said. "I have people at his home, watching. Still no sign of him. It may be time to check his roots."

"Meaning?"

"He's from a village in the Balochistan district. Probably coincidence, but we should check it, just the same. Unfortunately, I have no troops under my direct command to do the job."

"How many would you need?" Shabou inquired.

"No more than twenty, twenty-five."

"Colonel Dalal won't like that. It may start him asking questions," Shabou said.

Gazsi shrugged. "Let him perform the search, by all means. I have my hands full, as it is."

Shabou reached for a pen and pad of notepaper. "What is this village called?"

"Giri. You'll find it located northwest of Bela, sixty miles or so. It should be plotted on a decent military map."

"I'll pass this on. Meanwhile, how is the project after the disruption?"

"As you know, Deputy Minister, we managed to recover all the data the woman tried to smuggle from the laboratory. She had no chance to pass it on. I've increased security throughout the plant, and we're on schedule."

"Still two weeks for the delivery?" Shabou asked.

"*If* we have no further problems, I have been assured the deadline will be met."

"In that case, you must guarantee that there are no more problems, yes?"

Gazsi turned on an oily smile and said, "I live to serve, Deputy Minister."

"MY VILLAGE IS CALLED Giri. It has no translation that I ever learned," Pahlavi said.

"How do they deal with uninvited visitors?" Bolan asked.

"You'll be safe with me," the young man promised. "They will not harm you."

Bolan wasn't terribly concerned about the natives as a threat, though he could never rule it out completely. At the moment, he was more concerned about the danger he might pose to them. If they attacked him, he was bound to fight. And even if they didn't—

"Who knows where you come from?" Bolan asked.

"Excuse me?"

"It's a simple question. Who can trace you to your village? Anyone from Project X? The military or police?"

Pahlavi shook his head. "It isn't common knowledge. Certainly, no one from Project X should trace me there."

"Unless they asked your sister?" Bolan added.

"She would never tell—"

It hit Pahlavi then, and silenced him. Bolan drove on another mile or so, while Pahlavi ran through a mental slide show of horrific images, his sister trying not to answer vital questions from a gang of savages with drugs and wicked tools ready at hand. It was the kind of thing no brother should be forced to think about.

Bolan knew that, because he'd seen the savages at work, firsthand.

"She might have told them," Pahlavi said finally, speaking around a hard lump in his throat.

"Is that still where you want to go?" Bolan asked pointedly.

"There's nowhere else," Pahlavi answered. "I must warn them, even if we cannot stay there."

Bolan understood the need and didn't argue with it. He'd likely have done the same himself, under the same circumstances.

"What about gasoline?" he asked.

"They always have a stockpile in the village, for the tractor and the truck."

Both singular. It sounded like the kind of place a rifle company could level in an hour, maybe less if they had sappers with them and some plastique to complete the job. Bolan hoped that wouldn't happen—and that he wouldn't be dropped into the middle of it, if it did—but since Pahlavi was his only link to Project X, he felt obliged to ride along.

"We should be careful, going in," Bolan advised. "No matter how unlikely it may seem, the opposition could have someone waiting for you in the village. Maybe just a lookout to alert them, if you show your face, or maybe occupation troops. We can't take anything for granted."

"No," Pahlavi said. "I understand." He sounded hopeless now, as if the mental image of his sister's suffering had sapped his strength and will to fight.

"Remember," Bolan told him, "you can't change the past, but you can still affect the future. Project X is still a danger to your country and the world. Don't fade out on me now."

"I am not fading out, as you describe it," said Pahlavi, something like fire coming back into his voice. "It grieves me that my sister died because of me. You understand?"

"I've been there," Bolan answered. "What you need to bear in mind is that she made a choice. She was as strong and as committed as you are. She took a chance and lost. It happens. But it's not your fault. You couldn't do her part, inside the lab. She knew that, and she took it on herself."

"You're wrong about one thing," Pahlavi said. "Darice was not as strong as I am. She was many times stronger. It sickens me to think how much she must have suffered, buying time to let me and the others get away."

"Sick makes a decent starting place, if you don't let it ruin you," Bolan declared. "Take that and turn it into anger, then determination. Bear in mind that you can only pay the debt by living up to what she would expect from you. The men you want to punish can be hurt by tearing down all that they've built before they have a chance to profit from it."

"You are supposed to be a fighting man," Pahlavi said, "not a psychologist."

"Is there a difference?" Bolan asked him.

"Maybe not. I have no answer to such questions, anymore."

"How about ammunition?" Bolan asked, changing the subject. "Your Beretta must be running low."

Pahlavi drew his pistol, checked its load, then rummaged through his pockets. "I have nineteen cartridges remaining, and an empty magazine," he said.

"Check out the duffel bag behind my seat," Bolan suggested. "You should find some loose 9 mm rounds there, in boxes."

Twisting in his seat, Pahlavi did as he was told. A moment later, he faced front, a box of ammo with the pistol in his lap, and glanced sidelong at Bolan in the driver's seat.

"You came prepared for war," he said.

"I came prepared for almost anything," Bolan replied. "It's the best way to stay alive."

"Like your Boy Scouts," Pahlavi quipped, forcing a smile.

"Same notion," Bolan said. "Just all grown up."

"I fear there will be more killing," Pahlavi said.

Count on it, Bolan thought. "I wouldn't be surprised. You up for that?" he asked.

"I'll do what must be done. Give up my life, if necessary, to prevent a worse catastrophe."

"The dedication's good," Bolan observed, "but in my own experience, it's not the best idea to concentrate on dying all the time. It can become a self-fulfilling prophecy. You know the Green Berets' translation of the Golden Rule?"

Pahlavi frowned and shook his head.

"Do unto others," Bolan said, "before they do it unto you."

"I understand this, now. We do it to them big time, yes?"

"I hope so," Bolan answered, his mind divided between the open highway he could see and the invisible pitfalls that still lay somewhere up ahead.

It would be dark soon, helping to conceal them—or, perhaps, making them stand out more than ever on the highway, with no other traffic running in the same direction. Bolan hoped they wouldn't meet another army unit on their way, but anything was possible.

They would've found the dead by now, or Pahlavi's friends, at least, beside the road. The search would spread from there and follow them, unless someone from Project X already knew about Pahlavi's link to Ohm, and where he could be found if he was forced to hide.

What would be waiting for them when they reached Pahlavi's village, *if* they reached it?

Bolan didn't know, but he was going to find out.

And soon.

7

"Two more miles, I think," Pahlavi said. "I recognize that tree."

He pointed through the windshield to a massive, twisted oak tree on their left, some eighty yards ahead. It reminded Bolan of a giant from a fairy tale, chained and condemned to ever-lasting torture with its crooked, strangely angled limbs, most of them thicker than his body at the root. At closer range, Bolan could see the trunk was also scarred, as if by shrapnel or the manic hacking of an uncoordinated woodsman bent on maiming, rather than removing it.

He didn't ask, and put the sudden rush of grim, unbidden images out of his mind. Whatever had befallen this old tree in bygone days, it had nothing to do with him.

Pahlavi seemed to read his mind. As they passed the great, distorted oak, he said, "There was a battle here, around the time that I was born. Really a skirmish, I suppose you'd say. A pair of warlords fighting over territory, I believe. All dead, now, but they left their marks behind."

"Is that still going on?" asked Bolan.

"Not so much, here in Balochistan," Pahlavi said. "We still have bandits, kidnappers and such, but there are no great leaders like the old days that my papa used to talk about. If we went farther north, perhaps, into Azad Kashmir or the Northwest Frontier, we'd have a better chance of meeting private troops."

"Maybe some other time," Bolan replied. "Running from one army's enough for me."

"But you forget the men of Project X."

"Aren't they the same?" Bolan inquired.

"I've never been completely sure. Darice—" his voice still caught at mention of his sister's name "—mentioned that military men would sometimes come around the lab, but its security was managed by civilians led by Kurush Gazsi, formerly a member of the state security police."

"Former?" Bolan asked.

Pahlavi shifted in his seat, stared out the window at the passing countryside. "I've heard some stories about why he left. They vary, but most revolve around brutality toward women. I don't like to think... But what is done cannot be undone, yes?"

"Sometimes it can be punished," Bolan told him. "Getting even may be stretching it, but sometimes tabs get paid."

"I do not understand."

"Forget it. How much farther?"

"One mile, unless my memory has failed."

"When was the last time you were here?" Bolan inquired.

"Nearly five years ago." In answer to a glance from Bolan, he went on. "It's not so long. I have no family remaining here, but there are friends I trust."

I hope so, Bolan thought, remembering that trust could sometimes be misplaced. "No enemies?" he asked.

"Not that I know of," Pahlavi said, "but in times like these..." Another shrug.

Bolan tapped the Land Rover's brake and said, "We've still got time to turn around, try somewhere else. Once we're inside the village, it may be too late."

"No, we'll be safe," Pahlavi said, insistently. "From my people, at least."

Another qualifier, they were grating hard on Bolan's nerves. He eased off on the brake and drove ahead, regardless, following the narrow road that had branched off the highway six miles back. At least, he thought—or hoped—they'd be less likely to encounter military units on this route, the rough equivalent of a neglected one-lane county roadway in the States.

Or maybe not, if any kind of full-scale search was under way. The countryside might well be crawling with patrols, for all he knew, and overflights by spotter planes or helicopters could detect them just as readily as any watchers on the ground. More easily, in fact, if they had broadcast an alert.

The countryside had changed dramatically over the course of their long drive, from flatlands cloaked in scattered forests to rugged mountains, fading back to gently rolling hills. Geologists no doubt could've described the area's prehistory from what they saw around them, but the Executioner was more concerned with present-day events and what they held in store for him.

Like being caught up in some madman's scheme to launch a first-strike nuclear attack against his next-door neighbor, never thinking—or perhaps not caring—that the aftermath would leave his homeland a disaster area, unfit for human habitation in the present century. What would be gained from such insanity?

Did anybody ever simply stop and think?

"We're almost there," Pahlavi warned.

Bolan eased back on the accelerator, slowing through a long curve that revealed, at last, the first glimpse of a smallish village nestled in a vale with hills on either side. Smoke spiraled skyward from a dozen chimneys, and he picked out human figures moving on the one street he could see.

"Last chance to change your mind," he told Pahlavi.

"Trust me. I know what I'm doing."

Famous last words, Bolan thought, but he followed his guide's direction, rolling toward the village at a steady thirty miles per hour on the narrow road where grass sprouted through fissures in the pavement.

All movement in the village stopped as they drew closer, save for some inhabitants calling their children from the street, to go inside. A few adults stood waiting, watching, as the car approached. Pahlavi rolled his window down, as if to give them all a better look at him, but Bolan wasn't conscious of their attitude appreciably warming.

"There," Pahlavi told him, finally. "Pull over there, outside that store."

Bolan obeyed, parked parallel to the low curb and killed the engine. Feeling hostile eyes upon him, he kept one hand near the SIG-Sauer beneath his jacket.

"Here we are," Pahlavi said, smiling. "I'm home."

They sat in silence for a moment.

"Wait," Pahlavi said at last, and stepped out of the car.

Bolan remained behind the steering wheel, with one hand on or near his hidden pistol.

Standing in the street beside their vehicle, Pahlavi scanned the old, familiar facades of the shops and homes that lined the street. He breathed in the aromas from the bakery and from the kitchens where some women had already started preparation of their evening meals. There was no restaurant in Giri, and no industry to foul the air, but with a little effort he could smell farm animals, the ripe scent of manure that was never far away in an agricultural community.

Pahlavi focused on the people next, having supplied them with ample opportunity to study him. The nearest was an old woman he recognized, although his mind would not disgorge her name upon command. Pahlavi smiled at her regardless, greeting her with proper courtesy and turning toward a clutch of three men standing near the entrance to the bakery.

The youngest of them was a stranger to Pahlavi, but he knew the other two, both more or less his father's age, if only Haj Pahlavi had survived to middle age.

Pahlavi moved around the car, as he neared the men. His smile was cautious and reserved, befitting one who speaks to elders after many months away from home.

"Mr. Saldani. Mr. Kolda. It is good to see you both. I trust that you are well."

"Is this young Darius Pahlavi?" Kolda asked. Pahlavi couldn't tell if he was talking to the others or himself.

"It is," Pahlavi answered, then corrected it. "I am. It has been long since I returned to visit, but I often think of Giri and its people while I'm working in the city."

"You live in Karachi now," Mr. Saldani said, as if remembering some arcane bit of knowledge from the age before recorded language. "I remember that."

"You are correct," Pahlavi said.

"Who is the stranger in the car?" asked the younger man, stepping forward as if he would interpose himself between Pahlavi and the older men.

"I do not know your name," Pahlavi said. He judged the young man to be several years his junior, very early twenties at the most. "Perhaps, if we were introduced…"

"I am Asad Kalari. Will you answer me?"

Pahlavi turned deliberately from Kalari, toward the older men who knew him, answering to them out of respect. "My friend is an American. He comes to help me seek Darice, my sister, who has disappeared."

It was a lie, of course, but close enough to truth for conversation in that time and place. Asad Kalari fumed at being bypassed, while Saldani and Kolda nodded thoughtfully, considering his answer.

"She worked also in the city, I believe," Saldani said.

Pahlavi nodded. "That's correct."

"It is an evil place," Kolda said. "No man knows his neighbor. Vile habits proliferate."

"There is much truth in what you say," Pahlavi granted, nodding humbly.

"Would you bring those troubles back to Giri with you?" Kalari asked.

Once again, Pahlavi spoke past him, addressing those he knew from childhood. "I bring nothing with me but my history among you, and a friend who volunteered to help me in a time of difficulty. If it troubles anyone among you for us to remain—"

"It troubles me," Kalari said.

"Be quiet," Kolda ordered, and the younger man retreated, glowering in anger but too wise or frightened to rebel. Pahlavi knew he would bear watching if they stayed, and that he might be tempted to betray them even if they left immediately, though he couldn't understand the instant enmity that Kalari harbored.

"All sons of Giri may find welcome here," Saldani said. "It is too bad your parents are not here to greet you."

"I hope that they may guide me, nonetheless," Pahlavi said, "and help me find Darice."

"We have not seen her since the last time that you visited together," Kolda offered. "Some supposed that she had married in the city and would not be seen again."

"She was not—*is* not—married," Pahlavi said. "There was no man in her life."

Both older men stood silent for a moment, nodding in something like commiseration. "It is sometimes hard for young ones," Kolda said at last, "no matter where they live. But in the city, worst of all."

"With your permission," Pahlavi said, "I will introduce my friend."

"By all means, let us meet him," Saldani said.

Moving to the car, Pahlavi beckoned Bolan from the driver's seat, the older men watching the tall American unfold and turn to face them.

"Matthew Cooper," he began, "meet Bhaskar Kolda and Rohin Saldani, elders of our village."

"We are not so old," Saldani said, "as some would have you think."

"A pleasure," Bolan said to both of them, shaking the hands they offered, then returning to his place beside Pahlavi.

"We all have much to talk about," Saldani said. "Starting with why the two of you are wearing guns."

CAPTAIN SAHAN AMBIKA checked his watch and wondered how much longer it would be until they reached the peasant village. He resented being taken from the bandit hunt to search a clutch of hovels where he had no realistic hope of finding outlaws or guerrillas, but Ambika always followed orders.

The alternative was unacceptable.

His squad consisted of forty men besides himself, riding in two jeeps and two open trucks. The second jeep in line was equipped with a heavy machine gun, while his men all carried automatic rifles. He was confident that they could cope with any threat they might encounter in the countryside.

And yet—

Ambika knew—*had* known—Sachi Chandaka and believed he was a capable lieutenant. Still, somehow, Chandaka had been slaughtered with a complement of thirty men, supposedly by bandits he'd encountered on the highway. Now, Ambika was assigned to search the village that had spawned some radical reported missing from Karachi, as if that had anything to do with what was happening.

Ambika knew that nothing was impossible, and if his mission took him out of danger's way, he should be grateful. At the same time, though, he craved action, wishing that he could find the men responsible for wiping out Chandaka's company, punish the men in his own way for their crime against the peace and their grave insult to the Pakistani army.

"How much longer?" he demanded of his driver.

"We are nearing the coordinates, Captain," the soldier answered. "I have never been to Giri, so I do not recognize the landmarks, sir."

Of course not. No one he knew had ever been to Giri, Ambika thought. There were countless tiny villages scattered throughout the width and breadth of Pakistan, most of them represented only on the largest military maps, ignored by nearly everyone outside their own small settlements. Only in crisis or catastrophe did average Pakistanis hear about such villages, and having absorbed their fleeting tragedy, quickly forgot them once again.

But if Ambika found the slayers of his comrades in the Giri settlement, it would be long remembered as the place where they were slaughtered to the last man, without quarter. He would be the hero of the hour, suitably rewarded for his courage and his tactics on the battlefield.

Granted, headquarters wanted one of them alive, at least, to spill his guts for the interrogators and explain precisely why Chandaka's men where killed. Ambika would do everything within his power to obey those orders, but the lawless types rarely surrendered without some display of force. And once his men had tasted blood…

"Bring me a prisoner," Colonel Anish Dalal had ordered, "and I will remember you." That couldn't hurt an officer's career, but if the enemy was armed and stubbornly resisted all negotiations, what more could Ambika do?

Dalal would not be happy to receive news of another massacre…unless, perhaps, the dead this time were those who'd killed his soldiers earlier that day. A victory was always welcome, even more so after an embarrassing defeat. And who could say? Perhaps Captain Ambika *would* capture alive one of the men he sought.

For the moment, he concentrated on finding the village called Giri, where a small-time radical named Darius Pahlavi had first seen the light of day. Colonel Dalal had not been generous with details, as to why he sought Pahlavi, and Ambika had not dared to ask. The little he was told frankly confused him, double-talk about a group of scientists or enemies of science—he was not exactly sure—who somehow jeopardized the national security. The link between such matters and a bandit massacre of troops eluded him, but it was not his job to question orders from above. Only to follow them as closely as he could, while trying cautiously to grab some glory for himself.

That was the trick, he thought, advancing without stumbling over hidden obstacles or stepping into snares that others had prepared for him.

Thus far, Ambika had enjoyed a relatively smooth and prosperous career. He claimed awards and decorations, shared in certain graft that came his way—never ostentatiously—and generally brought credit to the service and himself. If he was not exactly loved by those in his command, neither was he despised like some who had been murdered by their own troops on patrol, or while they slept. Ambika tried to strike a happy medium, ensuring that his happiness came close behind that of his nominal superiors.

"Quarter of a mile," his driver said, remembering just in the nick of time to add the "sir."

Ambika shifted in his seat, trying to get a better view around the curve, but simple physics foiled his effort. Burning nervous energy, he drew the service pistol from his holster, jacked its slide to put a live round in the chamber, set the safety and returned the weapon to its place on his right hip.

Whatever happened in the village, he would not be unprepared.

A moment later, he could see the clutch of humble buildings ahead, shrouded in dusky shadows. Faint lights in a number of the windows told Ambika this was one more rural village with, at best, a rundown generator to provide erratic power—and perhaps it would have none.

Life in the Pakistani countryside was like that, sometimes. Something from the nineteenth century, or even from Medieval times—until the tricky bastards came up blasting with a new black-market automatic weapon.

Taking up his two-way radio, Captain Ambika spoke. "All troops. The village is in sight. Be on alert for any danger, but fire only on my order unless fired upon. Repeat, fire only on my order unless fired upon. Captain Ambika, out."

8

Bolan's spoon was poised halfway to his mouth, bearing another bite of savory lamb stew, when the alarm sounded. He didn't understand the words, but from the tone of voices calling in the street, he knew it had to be trouble. Bhaskar Kolda, seated at the same table with Bolan, Darius Pahlavi and Rohin Saldani, rose and swiftly moved to stand before an open window.

Bolan swallowed his stew, together with an urge to ask Pahlavi or his hosts exactly what the trouble was. They would explain it soon enough, he thought, and if the village elders weren't scrambling for guns, he might not need his own.

Kolda said something, turning from the window, and Pahlavi translated. "Soldiers."

This time, he had to ask. "How far away? How many?"

More fast talking between Kolda and Pahlavi, followed by a terse response to Bolan. "Four vehicles, with forty men, at least. They are outside the village and approaching."

Bolan pushed back from the dining table and drew the heavy duffel bag into his lap, but Kolda raised a hand as if to stop him, speaking earnestly in words that meant no more to Bolan than the sound of rain on shingles.

"Wait," Pahlavi translated. "He says there is a place for us to hide, while they inspect the village. We'll be safe."

"You really think so?"

"Such patrols are not unusual," Pahlavi said. "They come, ask questions, sometimes search the houses."

"That's a problem," Bolan said.

Kolda spoke rapidly, while Pahlavi nodded in understanding.

"We will not be in a house, but underneath it," Pahlavi said, rising from his chair. "Come, we must hurry now!"

Bolan swallowed his misgivings, rose and followed as the others left through a back door. Hidden from the view of any soldiers entering Giri by the main road, they passed along behind two houses, to another door where Kolda knocked, then entered without waiting for a summons.

Four new bodies made the small room crowded, since it already contained a family of five. Bolan immediately stopped and shook his head.

"Not here," he told Pahlavi. "There are too many civilians in the way."

"They have the best root cellar," Pahlavi said. "Also the best-hidden."

"Have him take us somewhere else," Bolan insisted. "Let us hide with him, instead of jeopardizing children."

"We will find no better place," Pahlavi argued, clearly trying not to shout in his excitement.

Even as they quarreled, Kolda and Saldani joined the master of the house in bending to a wall of paneling beneath a short, steep stairway to the attic. Bolan couldn't see the catch, but it was there, one skilled touch opening a trapdoor that was perfectly invisible when closed.

"Inside!" Pahlavi urged him. "We go downstairs now, and wait."

"You first," Bolan said, heedless of the look that passed across Pahlavi's face.

He didn't care much for the thought of dying underground, but if it had to happen, Bolan wouldn't be alone. And he most certainly would not be the first to make the hunched, scrabbling descent into strange darkness, while his guide and hosts remained above, ready to slam the trapdoor and imprison him.

At least, this way, if anything went wrong he'd have Pahlavi at his fingertips, a chance to snap his neck before the lights went out for good. It would be little consolation, at the end—but, then again, sometimes a little was enough.

Pahlavi blinked at Bolan, swallowed hard, then ducked and crawled in headfirst through the trap. He disappeared like Alice going down the rabbit's hole, and Bolan followed with his duffel bag of hardware, pausing in the narrow entryway to glance back at the others who remained behind.

He didn't speak their language, but he hoped that the expression on his face gave them some hint of his determination not to be entombed without a fight. It obviously wouldn't be the children's fault if anything went wrong, but as for Kolda and Saldani, if they should betray him, Bolan only hoped he'd have a chance to reach them one more time.

Below, Pahlavi used a penlight Bolan hadn't seen before to light the narrow, steeply sloping stairs. Someone behind him closed the trapdoor and he heard a latch engage. There'd be no problem blasting through it with his AKMS or the SIG-Sauer, if it came down to that, but if he had to go that route, the odds were good that well-armed enemies would open up the trapdoor first, and either lob grenades downstairs or spray the root cellar with automatic fire.

"Trust me," Pahlavi said, as Bolan reached his level and set down the duffel bag. "We will be safe here."

Bolan kept his face deadpan, replying, "Let's hope so."

"Regrettably," Pahlavi said, "I must turn off the light. In case they search the house, you understand?"

"I hear you," Bolan answered.

The man-made cave went dark.

PAHLAVI UNDERSTOOD the grim American's misgivings. Here he was, in a strange land, surrounded by people he didn't know, speaking a language that he couldn't understand. On top of that, enemy troops were closing on him for the second time within six hours, and his only hiding place was a hole in the ground, at the mercy of those very strangers whom he'd only met a short time earlier.

Pahlavi understood, but he had problems of his own. He wasn't exactly claustrophobic, but hiding underground was not his first choice, either. After switching off the meager light, it felt as if the walls were closing in on him, the ceiling dropping lower, squeezing all the air out of the cellar that might soon become their tomb.

For all his talk of safety, Pahlavi was not convinced that they could fool the military searchers. First, the men who hunted them were almost certainly inflamed by losing comrades to an unknown enemy. They were empowered under law to search most places without warrants or permission of the owners. If they started ripping homes apart, what were the odds that they would find the hidden trapdoor, he wondered.

Pahlavi pocketed the penlight, and drew the sleek Beretta semiauto pistol from beneath his jacket. It was primed and fully loaded, with the safety off.

Why bother? Why risk any extra noise? He thought.

Pahlavi heard the soft sound of a zipper, followed by metallic sounds as Cooper drew his automatic rifle from the duffel bag. The American didn't ask for light. He obviously could prepare and check his weapon by its feel alone.

Pahlavi knew he would be trapped alone underground, with the American if he decided that he'd been betrayed.

That knowledge made Pahlavi's skin crawl, but he countered it with a reminder to himself that he and the American were allies, pledged to the same mission. If he gave no indication of betraying him, did not play him false, there was no cause for the American to harm him.

Upstairs, Pahlavi heard footsteps and muffled voices, sounding as if they came from a hundred yards away, through walls of cotton batting. He made no attempt to eavesdrop, knowing it would be impossible from where he stood. If he should climb the stairs and press his ear against the trapdoor panel, possibly he could decipher what was said, but he would also place himself at greater risk.

A nagging doubt, the product of cramped quarters and pitch-darkness, wormed its way into Pahlavi's mind. What if his old father's friends Kolda and Saldani had decided to betray him after all? Perhaps a large reward was offered for the men who'd killed so many soldiers, or the villagers simply might wish to spare themselves from harm during the search.

It would be simple. Just a word to the commander of the search party, a finger pointed from the threshold toward the attic stairs and the trapdoor beneath. There'd be a rush of heavy boots across the floor above his head, and by the time Pahlavi was positioned to defend himself, crowbars and axes would be hacking at the access panel. Seconds later, he and Cooper would be fatally exposed to searchlights, gunfire, anything the soldiers chose to use.

A sudden terrifying image of a flamethrower erupted in Pahlavi's mind and brought a cold sweat to his forehead. More than cramped, dark places, he abhorred the thought of death by fire. Could he stand fast and fight, while flames gnawed at his flesh and stripped it from his bones?

A wave of nausea left him trembling, but he kept his supper down with a determination that surprised him. More than courage, it was fear of being shamed in front of Cooper—even now, when the American could catch no glimpse of him—that gave Pahlavi any hint of strength. Pride countered terror, and if that was what it took to steel his nerves, so be it.

There came a sound of rumbling vehicles outside, more a vibration through the earth itself than any auditory tone. Above Pahlavi, more footsteps told him that Kolda and Saldani had gone out to meet the soldiers, followed by the tenants of the house. He pictured the inhabitants of Giri, lined up in the street, facing the new arrivals with a combination of beleaguered innocence and thinly veiled hostility. They would know how to play that scene.

All that Pahlavi had to think about was its conclusion, whether it would be a death scene for himself and Cooper or a near-miss, leaving them alive and free to fight another day.

Clutching his pistol in both hands, so tightly that his knuckles ached, Pahlavi stared into the darkness, waiting for a sound that would reveal the presence of his enemies directly overhead. That would be the signal to assume his place beneath the stairs and aim in the direction of the trapdoor, ready to start shooting at the first blow of the ax.

When that time came, Pahlavi hoped he wouldn't stumble over Cooper's duffel bag or run into the man himself. If he had to die here, like a cornered animal, he hoped to manage it with some shred of his dignity intact.

And take some of the soldiers with him when he fell.

9

Captain Ambika was determined that the search of Giri village would be thorough. Never mind that he believed the task assigned to him was both demeaning and a waste of time. He would exert himself the same way as if he had been called to rescue the prime minister himself. No clue would be ignored, no stone unturned. Ambika would use every trick he knew, in order to succeed.

And that was bad news for the peasants standing in his path.

Ambika kept a firm hand on his holstered pistol as they rolled into the village, even though he doubted whether any of the peasants would resist. There were guerrillas in the countryside, no doubt about it, but they wouldn't be in Giri—or, if so, they wouldn't jeopardize their sanctuary by provoking skirmishes with troops. It would require a special goad to make the traitors drop their masks.

Like turning up an arms cache in the village, for example, then arresting those who kept it on a treason charge.

A group of peasants came to meet Ambika on the street, the men in front, their women hanging back with children clutched against their skirts. Ambika took his time surveying them before he stepped down from the jeep and moved to face them.

One of them, apparently the village elder, ducked his head

beneath a faded turban, not quite bowing to Ambika, flicking glances at Ambika's rank insignia.

"Captain," the man said, "how may we be of service to you?"

"I am seeking out a nest of traitors," Ambika said, voice raised so that all could hear him. "And one traitor in particular. This afternoon, a government patrol was ambushed and destroyed. Two of the men responsible are dead. The others passed this way."

It was a total lie, for all Ambika knew, but it was necessary to command the respect of the villagers. He could not do that with vague generalities. Above all, he would not permit them to believe that they were safe, objects of mere peripheral concern. They had his full attention for the moment, and Ambika would have theirs.

"We know nothing of any incidents," the village spokesman said.

"Nothing? No incidents at all?" Ambika mocked him. "Life in Giri must be very dull indeed."

The man blinked at him, as if confused, then said, "We mind our business, Captain, and respect authority."

"I have no doubt about the first part, anyway," Ambika said. "As to the other, I must satisfy myself. Does no one here know Darius Pahlavi?"

There was stirring in the crowd, but only silence in response until the man said, "He lived here as a child."

"And comes no more?" Ambika challenged.

Answered with a shrug. "No, sir."

Ambika scanned the faces, looking for a nervous liar, then declared, "We shall begin to search at once for fugitives and contraband. Cooperation is required. Resistance will be punished. Am I understood?"

The man ducked his head again, but made no verbal answer. Rather than compel him to reply, Ambika turned to face his men, raised one hand overhead and whipped it through a short, circular motion, as if twisting an invisible crank. At once, his troops began unloading from their jeeps and trucks in a dramatic rush, boots stamping, weapons rattling.

"I say again," he told the huddled villagers, voice raised to reach the homes around them, "we are here to search this village. Any contraband or fugitives discovered will result in charges being filed. I may feel generous, however, if such individuals or items are surrendered now, thus saving us the effort of pursuing them."

Dead silence met his suggestion. With a shrug, Ambika turned and told his men, "One-third of you remain with me. The rest, split up and start the search from each end of the village, working toward the middle. First, the north side of the road, then cross and do the south side. Make a thorough job of it and use all necessary force."

A pair of sergeants organized the teams and sent them off to carry out Ambika's orders, while the captain waited by his jeep, watching. His comment about "necessary force" gave them the nod to ransack any shop or dwelling as they liked, crash doors and ransack cupboards, trampling all the contents underfoot.

Ambika had no realistic hope of finding much beyond a little hashish and a few stray guns, but he was going through the motions with a vengeance. None of his superiors could look back, later, and pretend that he had coasted on this job, tackling the exercise with anything but absolute commitment.

It was hard on Giri's residents, of course, but life was always hard on peasants. How else would they learn their proper place and hold to it when they felt stirrings of rebellion deep inside?

In truth, although they did not recognize the fact, Ambika thought he would be doing them a favor when his soldiers tore their shops and homes apart. A little inconvenience now could save a world of grief later, in case they harbored any notions of consorting with traitors and rising against the regime.

Ambika watched as doors were kicked in at the far ends of the village, to his left and right. His soldiers likely would not try the knobs to find out if they were unlocked. Sweeps like the present one acquired their own momentum, often led to certain excesses if a commander didn't keep a sharp eye on his men. Ambika had no tolerance for rape or outright looting, but if his troops roughed up a few stray villagers, he saw no harm in that.

Ambika reckoned peasants were undisciplined and lazy, as a rule. It was his duty, as a military officer, to teach them all the error of their ways. And if those errors should include some kind of criminal activity, no matter how mundane or trivial, he was obliged to punish it.

Beginning now.

THE STOUT FLOOR OVER Bolan's head echoed with tramping footsteps, as invaders worked their way around the house. At one point, dust rained down into his face and made him step away and move closer to the stairs he couldn't see. A faint shuffling beside him indicated that Pahlavi had done likewise.

The sounds from upstairs were muted and distorted in the cellar. Voices hardly carried through the floor at all, while the report of heavy objects falling echoed through the chamber underground, as if Bolan was standing on the inside of a massive kettledrum.

He heard the soldiers slinging furniture around, pictured the humble dining table and its ring of simple chairs. The sound of smashing crockery made Bolan grit his teeth. It would be such an easy thing, he thought, to rush upstairs, surprise the soldiers at their ruthless work and drop them where they stood.

But what would happen next?

He guessed there would be two or three troopers assigned to the house, while the rest searched elsewhere or watched from the street, held back in reserve. At the first show of resistance, their commander would be ready to pounce with full force.

And how much was that?

Bolan had glimpsed two trucks, with two jeeps leading, and there might be more behind. Assuming that he'd seen it all, there could be fifty soldiers in the village. They'd all have automatic weapons and presumably know how to use them. Even if the Executioner could drop them all, with or without Pahlavi's help, the enemy would still have ample time and opportunity to slaughter some of Giri's residents.

The risk was unacceptable.

Bolan would fight if forced to, if his enemies discovered the trapdoor and charged downstairs, but he would not provoke a massacre simply to keep his hosts from losing plates or furniture.

Pahlavi, on the other hand, was getting antsy. Bolan couldn't see him, but he felt the Pakistani standing close beside him, shifting restlessly from one foot to the other, breathing heavily. He wasn't hyperventilating yet, but if he kept it up, he might get there. Bolan reached out for him and gripped his shoulder, felt Pahlavi flinch and gasp.

Leaning across to him, Bolan whispered in the general direction of his ear, "Calm down. You blunder into this, you'll only make things worse."

He felt Pahlavi nod and hoped his words had gotten through the rush of nervous energy. There would be guilt, too, he imagined, feeling how Pahlavi trembled underneath his hand. By now, the Pakistani had to be thinking that his journey home for comfort hadn't been the best of his ideas.

Perhaps it was a lesson that Pahlavi should have learned the first time, when his sister disappeared. In some respects, he was a stranger in his homeland now, hunted by soldiers. Bolan wondered how much punishment the people of Giri would absorb before they cut their losses and betrayed him, and the stranger he had brought into their midst.

The upstairs search had swept past the hidden trapdoor and was moving into the small home's remaining rooms. More crashing, banging sounds reverberated through the floor. It sounded as if the invaders were deliberately wrecking everything that they could reach.

Bolan knew precisely how they felt, those hostile men in uniform. He'd been there, after losing friends in combat, suddenly confronted with civilians who most likely fed his enemies at every opportunity, their expressions stopping just short of defiance. And a soldier *knew* that when he turned his back the peasants would be grinning, laughing to themselves about his comrades who had died in agony, beset by fear.

It was an easy thing to act on impulse, punish those available instead of those who pulled the triggers. By the time the smoke cleared, an embarrassed warrior might convince himself they were one and the same.

But no gunshots echoed through the rooms upstairs, and after several more moments, the tramping boots retreated, exiting into the street. More homes to search, more families to terrorize. Beside him in the darkness, Darius Pahlavi slowly let his pent-up breath escape like air leaking out of a punctured tire.

Bolan stood fast, knowing the noisy exit could've been a

trick. Suppose their hosts had pointed to the trapdoor early on, or in their last extremity. What would prevent some of the soldiers from departing ostentatiously, while one or more remained upstairs, automatic rifles pointed at the door. The others could be waiting in the street, to rush back in at the report of gunfire. Bolan would not risk it. Better to remain exactly where they were until Pahlavi's friends came back to signal that the coast was clear.

He found an earthen wall and leaned against it, not relaxing for a moment his firm grip upon the AKMS rifle.

Pahlavi's palms were sweating, where they clutched his pistol, and he took turns wiping them against his pants. Never once did he consider letting down his guard, slipping the heavy weapon back inside his belt. It might be needed any moment, in case the soldiers doubled back to check for any hiding place they might have missed.

Pahlavi was concerned. There he was, in his own village, with his people all around him, and he'd brought them danger, pain and suffering.

Pahlavi would not blame them if they turned against him. Some of them were probably considering betrayal. The young man whom they'd met upon arrival, who had visibly disliked Pahlavi at a glance—Asad Kalari.

Would he be the one to spill the secret and reveal them to the enemy? What would become of young Kalari in the village if he did so. Once upon a time, Pahlavi knew, a traitor to his people would have been eliminated swiftly, ruthlessly. Kalari's own father would have been first to wield the knife, to purge his family's shame.

But now?

Pahlavi wasn't certain that he had a single true friend left in Giri—or, if there had been some to begin with, whether any would remain after the havoc being wrought above ground. It was easy to convince himself that everything the soldiers did to his people had to be his fault. The invaders were looking for him, after all, and for the tall American who sheltered with him in the basement.

Still, they might have come to Giri even if Pahlavi hadn't. It was probable, in fact. A massacre of soldiers was like slapping at a hornet's nest. Survivors swarmed in search of targets, seeking someone who would bear responsibility. A scapegoat would suffice, if they could not locate the guilty parties.

And while he, Pahlavi, stood in darkness waiting for the soldiers to withdraw, what had become of Project X?

It would be moving forward, drawing closer to the day when madmen pushed a button and the whole subcontinent went up in bright, irradiated flames. The moment when society as he had known it ceased to be, when even peasants in a tiny rural village would suffer from the lethal plague of modern science.

Pahlavi knew he had to survive this day, in order to direct Matt Cooper and unleash him on the enemies of sanity before they launched a global war to satisfy their twisted egos. If that meant he could not help his people at this moment of their glaring need, so be it.

But it pained him brutally, humiliated him and left Pahlavi feeling impotent. That, in and of itself, was nearly adequate to overthrow all common sense, fling caution to the wind and send him charging up the stairs to meet his enemies with pistol fire.

It would be suicide, of course, and while Pahlavi had considered something of the sort after his sister was taken from him, yielding to the guilt of having failed so miserably to protect her, he could not allow himself to harbor such ideas.

Self-pity was a luxury that he could not afford.

How much longer? he asked himself.

How long could it take a troop of soldiers to completely search a village of Giri's size? One hour? Two? Beyond that, he supposed the search would qualify as simple vandalism, aimed at punishing the locals for the simple act of knowing Darius Pahlavi.

He would pay them back somehow. Pahlavi vowed it to himself. If he survived this night and made it through his mission alive, Pahlavi would return and settle with his people, even if they should demand his final drop of blood.

It would be worth it, then, to regain their respect. He would have nothing left to prove, no one to please. There was no wife, no children, and no sister now to share Pahlavi's life. But for the task he had set himself, he would be hard pressed for a reason to go on.

But Cooper needed him alive. As an interpreter and guide, for insight into Pakistan and the nightmare of Project X. If he was killed this night, Cooper would be adrift—if not exactly helpless, then at least severely handicapped, he thought.

And what of Ohm? Would it go on without him? Did he even care?

He'd led two of the small group's members to their death that very afternoon and couldn't shake the guilt of it, although he knew that soldiers died in war. It had not been his plan to start a war. His enemies had done that, when they killed his sister, and now the hunting dogs were snuffling avidly along his trail.

Pahlavi hoped they would not find him where he hid this night. He needed time to settle old accounts and new ones, pay his debts before he went to face the final reckoning.

With Cooper at his side, Pahlavi was surprised to find that thought less frightening than when it first occurred to him some weeks earlier.

Losing Darice had stripped Pahlavi of his greatest single fear. The rest was all peripheral, his own life valued only with regard to what he must achieve before he died.

And thinking of his sister, of his people on the street somewhere above his head, Pahlavi reckoned one of his accomplishments should be revenge.

10

Ambika's men were halfway through their search of houses on the south side of the street, with nothing much to show for it. So far, they'd found an old bolt-action rifle and two shotguns, all presumably employed in hunting for the village stewpot. If his troops found nothing else, Ambika had decided he would take the weapons with him, make examples of their owners with a special punishment.

He had the three homes marked in mind already, but he hoped they would find something more substantial in the houses that were yet unsearched. Perhaps the fugitive Pahlavi, or a nice fat cache of weapons that would make the exercise worthwhile.

An outburst from a nearby house drew his attention from the thoughts that troubled him. Ambika turned in time to see two of his soldiers drag a struggling peasant through the open door and shove him down on all fours, in the street. When he tried bouncing back up, one of the soldiers kicked the man in the buttocks, keeping him off balance. As the angry peasant turned, still on his knees, he found two automatic rifles leveled at his face.

Just then, a third soldier emerged from the same house, carrying two assault rifles. One was his own standard-issue CETME, the other a Russian-made Kalashnikov. Ambika couldn't tell the caliber or model without looking closer, but it was a momentary lift, knowing that he had finally uncovered something that could pass for evidence of criminal activity.

Machine guns were as common as stray dogs in western Pakistan, although their sale was technically illegal. By some curious procedure that Ambika did not understand, police and prosecutors managed to ignore the countless vendors selling weapons to civilians nationwide, then voiced their shock when those same arms were used in ethnic feuding or, as earlier that very day, against the symbols of authority. Ambika would have tried a very different tack in that respect, but no one had requested his opinion or advice. Until they did, he was obliged to follow orders and do what he could to stem the tide of violence he witnessed every day.

Ambika moved with long strides toward the kneeling peasant, who had given up on fighting and tried to plead his case. The rifle was for self-defense and hunting, he insisted. He was not a criminal, had never broken any laws.

"The fact that you own this," Ambika told him, reaching out for the Kalashnikov, "is in itself a crime. You must have known that when you purchased it."

"Purchased?" The peasant wore a look of wounded innocence. "I found it by the roadside, Captain. I cannot afford to buy a weapon of this sort."

"And when you *found* it, did you not report your strange discovery to the police?" Ambika asked.

"There are no telephones in Giri, Captain."

"And, of course, you never see patrolmen on their rounds."

"Sir, by that time, I was afraid of what would happen if I spoke to the authorities. Who would believe me," the peasant asked, "when a wise man such as you does not?"

"A cruel dilemma," Ambika said. "But you could have left

the rifle where you found it, or gone back and put it there again, when it began to trouble you."

"I was afraid, Captain! If I did that, it might encourage someone else to take the gun and start a life of crime."

Ambika smiled, beginning to enjoy himself. "So, you've been keeping it at home, I understand, as something of a service to your country? A deterrent not only to crimes against yourself, but to prevent some other innocent from falling into error?"

"Yes!" The peasant flashed a beaming, hopeful smile. "That's it exactly! You *are* wise!"

"I'm wise enough, at least," Ambika said, "that I do not believe the pig's shit spewing from your liar's tongue."

"But Captain—"

"Silence! You are plainly guilty of a serious offense. The disposition of your case is up to me. I cannot go back to my colonel empty-handed and pretend I found no villains in this nest of crime." Ambika paused, then stepped in closer, lowering his voice. "But if you help me, there's a possibility I might forget to take you with me, or to name you in my field report."

The peasant glanced around to see if any of his fellow villagers were close enough to hear. "What must I do?" he whispered.

"Tell me where to find the rebel Darius Pahlavi. If you do this, I will take him in your place, and your transgression of the law shall be forgotten."

Hope flared in the peasant's eyes, but only for a moment. Then his shoulders slumped, a shadow seemed to pass across his face, and with a look of bitter resignation, shook his head.

"I cannot help you, Captain."

"Cannot, or will not?"

"It is all the same," the peasant said, almost weeping.

"The choice is yours. Perhaps interrogation back at headquarters will change your mind." Ambika turned to the young soldiers standing nearest him and said, "Arrest this man. And burn his house."

The peasant wailed as he was dragged toward the trucks. Behind Ambika, windows shattered and a soldier disappeared inside the captive's shabby home. When he emerged a moment later, dark smoke billowed out behind him, wafting skyward.

Ambika waited, let the flames begin to feed, then turned to face the other villagers. Raw hatred radiated from a ring of deadpan faces, showing only in their eyes.

"I have discovered one felon among you," Ambika said. "When I have a chance to question him in private, we'll return to claim the rest. You have one final chance to save yourselves by giving up the traitor Darius Pahlavi."

To his left, a young man seemed about to speak, had taken one step forward, when an older peasant struck him from behind. The young man fell, writhing, gasping in pain. Ambika saw the older man clutching a bloody knife.

A shot rang out, and the older man collapsed, blood spilling from a bullet wound above one eye. Ambika rounded on the soldier who had fired, enraged.

"Are you insane?" he shouted. "I needed that man alive. Expect a court-martial for this!"

He snatched the soldier's rifle, took it with him as he crossed the narrow street to kneel beside the young man who'd been stabbed. "What did you wish to tell me?" Ambika asked.

Struggling to speak, lips drawn back from his teeth in agony, the wounded man made several gasping, gargling sounds, then hacked a spray of crimson toward the captain's boots and died.

Ambika rose and stood above the man his careless soldier had dispatched. Kicking the corpse, he told the crowd, "I want to know where this one lived. No answer? Very well. If no one knows which home was his, we'll have to burn them all."

It took another moment, but a man of middle age stepped forward from the crowd, cheeks glistening with sweat or tears. Captain Ambika couldn't tell exactly which, nor did he care.

"You have something to say?" he challenged.

"There," the peasant told him, pointing toward a house at the west end of Giri's single street. "Kalari lived there."

"Burn it," Ambika snapped the order to no one in particular, and waited for his soldiers to respond. When the small house was burning merrily, he called out to the peasant crowd, "We're going now, but only for a short while. When we come again, all of your rotten secrets will be known."

BOLAN STOOD IN THE MIDDLE of the road, smoke drifting lazily around him from the ruins of two homes. Giri's inhabitants had fought with pails of sand and water to prevent the flames from spreading and had won that fight, but at a cost.

The bodies—Bhaskar Kolda and Asad Kalari—had been carried off the street and out of sight. Bolan could feel the villagers staring at him with frank hostility, while he stood waiting for Pahlavi to complete his whispered conversation with Rohin Saldani and a couple of the other elders. Finally, the young man shook their hands and doubled back to join him.

"I have promised to return," Pahlavi said, "and help rebuild the homes that were destroyed. It may not matter, though. The soldiers threatened to return and raze the village once they're finished questioning the prisoner."

"You know him, too?"

Pahlavi nodded. "All my life."

"You want to get him back?" Bolan asked. "If we play our cards right, maybe we can fix it so the soldiers don't come back."

Those soldiers, anyway, he thought, but kept the negative addendum to himself.

"What must we do?" Pahlavi asked.

"First thing, find out where someone stashed our wheels," Bolan replied.

Their car had not been visible when Bolan and Pahlavi left the root cellar, and he saw nowhere in the town that the searchers could have missed.

"I already have that answer," Pahlavi said. "There's a gully not so far away, choked full of weeds and shrubbery. Mr. Saldani hid it there, while we were underground."

"All right," Bolan said. "So, we get it back and follow the parade. I don't suppose you'd know a shortcut that would put us out in front of them? Something our car could handle without four-wheel drive?"

Pahlavi smiled, a weak effort, but better than the bleak expression he'd been wearing since they'd left the cellar hideout. "There is one way, yes," he answered. "Whether we can do it fast enough to intercept them is another question. And once doing so…"

He didn't need to finish the thought. There was a decent chance that catching up to the retreating soldiers could be suicide. Pahlavi thought he owed his people something, though, and Bolan didn't feel inclined to disagree.

"All right," he said again. "Let's roll."

11

Captain Ambika felt no remorse. Driving away from Giri, leaving two men dead and two homes burned, he wondered if he might have been too lenient. Still, if he'd shot more peasants, torched more homes without direct proof of involvement in some criminal activity, there was a chance—however slim—that his reaction might have had some adverse impact on the course of his career.

If nothing else, he had fulfilled the expectation of his colonel. He was bringing back a prisoner, albeit one detained for a relatively trivial offense. Perhaps they would get lucky, though, and scientific tests would trace the confiscated rifle to the slaughter of his comrades. Then Ambika's star would truly shine, and he'd be sent back to the village with an overwhelming force of men and armored vehicles to arrest the population en masse or kill them all and burn their village to the ground.

In either case, a victory like that would be a giant feather in Ambika's cap. He could be credited with solving an explosive mystery *and* bringing terrorists to bloody justice, all at the same time. Short of a combat field promotion during wartime, he was unaware of any other Pakistani army officer who had done more within a shorter time to help his country and himself.

Ambika caught himself building castles in the air and was instantly embarrassed. He swiped away the mental image of medals and parades with a wave of his hand. His driver saw it, peering at him closely.

"Sir?"

"It's nothing. Just a fly. Drive on and watch the road."

"Yes, sir."

Watch that, Ambika warned himself. If rumors spread that he was "funny," prone to strange gestures and private conversations with himself, he'd soon wind up in therapy and out of uniform completely. There was no road to advancement through insanity, unless the crazy one controlled a nation and could write his strange whims into law.

Not yet, Ambika thought, and stopped the budding smile before it cracked his grim facade.

The rugged hills flanking the highway cast long shadows in his path, reminding the captain that nightfall would soon be upon them. It had been a long day, but very productive. He had a story and a prisoner for Colonel Dalal. If ordered to remain on duty through the night, Ambika was prepared to do so. He would even drive back out to Giri for a dawn raid on the traitor's nest, if that was his assignment.

He'd do anything, in fact, to earn the rank and the authority he craved.

Ambika checked his watch and saw that they were still two hours from headquarters. He had considered calling in, to tell Dalal that he was coming with a prisoner, but then decided nothing would be gained by that. There was no urgency, no other identified offenders still at large for other squads to chase.

He would arrive, present the gift, then wait as patiently as possible for his superior's reaction. With a little luck—

Ambika heard a sound like a backfire, maybe from the jeep

behind them, but a backfire wouldn't crack the windshield of Ambika's vehicle or make his driver slump over the steering wheel. Blood seeped from a throat wound while the driver gasped and gargled, raising both hands from the wheel to grasp his ruptured neck.

"For God's sake, don't!" Ambika shouted.

Ambika lunged to grasp the steering wheel, just as a second bullet pierced the windshield, punching through his driver's head. The man slid lower in his seat, his right foot jammed on the accelerator even as he died.

The jeep surged forward, revving hard until its lifeless driver failed to shift the gears. Ambika couldn't reach the clutch pedal, but he hung on to the steering wheel as if his life depended on it.

Which, he well knew, it might.

Swerving, the jeep veered off the road, rumbled across the shoulder and began to climb the nearest hill. Ambika knew he couldn't make it, not with a dead man's feet blocking the accelerator and the clutch, but he fought hard to keep the vehicle from turning over as it climbed, still veering sharply to the left.

No brakes, no shift, and in the background he could hear more gunfire, automatic bursts, as the column was engaged. Ambika didn't understand exactly what was happening, but he knew it was bad.

And it was only getting worse.

The jeep stalled with a growling splutter, died, then started retreating, rolling slowly backward, down the hill.

Directly toward the narrow road that had become a battlefield.

BOLAN SHOT the driver of the lead jeep first in the hope his vehicle would stall and block the road, but somehow it had veered away and left the highway unimpeded, forcing him to try again.

It had been touch-and-go, racing the army column on a shortcut that Pahlavi had suggested, cutting corners while the main road curved away and back again to reach its destination. There were times when he thought his rented sedan would shake itself to pieces, but it put them on the spot ahead of their intended targets, leaving Bolan and Pahlavi separated from the main road by a range of rocky hills.

From there, they'd had to climb and scramble, Bolan weighted with the duffel bag of hardware, sometimes sliding in their haste, scraping the flesh from palms and knees. They'd found their places, one on each side of the road, just as the convoy rolled out of the dusk, dark toy-sized vehicles expanding by the heartbeat into the approach.

Then the battle began. The first two shots from Bolan's AKMS scored solid hits, albeit failing to achieve his goal. He compensated, put the lead jeep out of mind as it began a climb to nowhere on his left. The second jeep was slowing, the driver and his shotgun rider following the point vehicle with their eyes, while in the back a short machine gunner manned his weapon.

Bolan shot the gunner, a double tap that slammed him backward, away from his gun, and ended with a tumbling backward somersault out of the jeep. The shotgun rider produced an automatic rifle from the shadowed space between his feet and started firing toward the nearest hills. He didn't have a target yet, but he was trying, and the Executioner would give him points for that.

Points, and a quick, clean death.

Bolan squeezed off a burst that raked the soldier's chest and tore the rifle from his grasp. The impact of those bullets slammed his target hard into the driver, setting off a chain reaction as the jeep swerved. The driver tried to save it, working

the pedals and gearshift, but Bolan drilled his cheek beneath
the right rim of his helmet, already tracking toward another
target as the jeep began a lazy roll, disgorging bodies left and
right.

Both trucks stopped dead in the road, with soldiers
spilling from the beds and cabs. Some of them had a rough
fix on their enemy's position, firing toward the point where
Bolan crouched behind a boulder, partly hidden in a gully.
Their bullets whined and whistled in the air around him,
none yet close enough to make him worry, but it wouldn't
be much longer until some of them, at least, found their
mark and range.

So far, he hadn't glimpsed the prisoner they were hoping to
rescue, didn't have a clue what he would look like beyond
being out of uniform. Pahlavi knew the man, but they were separated by distance, swarming soldiers and the roaring sound of
automatic weapons. The best Bolan could do was watch out for
civilians and try not to spray the trucks so indiscriminately that
he hit a captive left inside.

But it was tough covering a force of forty-odd hostiles, even
when he had disposed of four or five in the first seconds of the
skirmish. All of the men were trained, to some degree, and even
if their standard action consisted of rousting unarmed villagers, some of them had to have dealt with bandits and guerrillas on the firing line. They didn't have the look of green
recruits, and they were more at home than the Executioner on
the present battleground.

He palmed a frag grenade, and then thought better of it. Explosives and shrapnel were both indiscriminate killers. He
couldn't lob grenades downrange without taking a risk that he
might kill or wound the man they'd come to rescue. A civilian,
yet, who wasn't part of the resistance, and who hadn't signed

a pledge to risk his life in combat for the cause. He might not recognize Pahlavi if they passed each other on the street, and by Pahlavi's own admission had no knowledge of the do-or-die campaign to frustrate Project X.

Pulling the hostage out would be a show of good faith to Pahlavi's village, nothing more or less. It wouldn't help their mission in the least, but could do it a world of harm if one or both of them were nailed by soldiers fighting for their lives.

Determined not to let that happen, Bolan risked a look around the boulder, tracking with his AKMS as he sought another target on the killing field.

PAHLAVI SPUTTERED as a bullet hit the ground in front of him, kicking a burst of sand into his face. He tasted grit, resisted the urge to spit it out, and focused rather on the action that unfolded right in front of him.

His first shot had gone wild after he jerked the pistol's trigger, missed the soldier he was aiming for and struck the left-rear fender of the second truck in line. It was a wonder anyone had even noticed, in the riotous confusion of the moment, but one of the troopers saw or heard it strike, projected its flight path to calculate a point of origin, and fired a burst in answer that had come uncomfortably close.

Pahlavi had to stop that soldier before he made a better shot or rallied his companions for a charge across the roadway. Blinking back tears from sand-stung eyes, Pahlavi steadied his Beretta in both hands and squeezed the trigger once again, with all the grim deliberation he could muster.

It worked.

His bullet caught the soldier roughly in the solar plexus, stole his wind and left him doubled over as if he was suffering a sudden bout of nausea. Instead of vomit, though, the wounded soldier spit a stream of blood across his own boots, then collapsed, twitching through the final moments of his life.

Pahlavi barely thought about it as he swept the field, seeking other targets. He was also watching for Jalil Yamuna, taken from the village by these soldiers, but as yet there'd been no sign of him.

Assuming he was bound for transport to the nearest army base, Pahlavi guessed they wouldn't drag Yamuna from the truck while they were fighting for their lives. He was, at best, a piece of excess baggage who would slow them down when speed was paramount. They'd figure it was better to leave him in the truck—whichever one it was—and if a bullet found him in the meantime, it was no great loss.

Survival was the soldiers' first priority, as it was for Pahlavi himself. He lacked their training but had already survived a battle against odds he would have previously labeled hopeless. Pahlavi hoped he might outlast another troop of enemies.

With Cooper firing from the far side of the trucks, most of the soldiers hurried to take cover on Pahlavi's side. It gave him an impressive field of targets—more than he could handle with the only weapon he possessed, in fact—but if they focused most of their attention on the sniper who appeared to threaten them the most, Pahlavi knew he had a chance to take them by surprise.

He wormed along the ditch that sheltered him, shifting positions from his former firing nest. When he had covered forty feet or so, Pahlavi stopped and chose another target, sighting down the barrel of his handgun, a man he'd never seen before fixed in the stark white outline of his sights.

Pahlavi waited for a blaze of firing from the soldiers, saw his target start to rise and squeezed his trigger gently. The pistol recoiled, buffeting against his palm, and Pahlavi's target stiffened, spine bowed by the bullet's impact. The man collapsed to one knee, groping backward with both hands to reach the wound he couldn't find, too late to stop the spout of crimson pouring from his back into the dust.

Pahlavi could've fired again and guaranteed the kill, but he was short on ammunition as it was and had too many targets still unscathed before him to be wasting mercy shots on anyone. He pivoted, his elbows braced on sand and gravel, sighting on the next soldier in line.

The man in olive drab was gaping at his stricken comrade, bending to shake the dying soldier, maybe asking what was wrong. Pahlavi took advantage of the momentary lapse and shot him through the left side of his chest.

The soldier slumped backward, a stunned expression on his face, and glanced down at the wet stain spreading across his shirt. Pahlavi didn't wait to see what happened next, already scuttling back along the ditch in the direction he had come from, looking for another vantage point, another chance to kill.

CAPTAIN AMBIKA ROLLED out of his jeep and spent a moment belly-down in sand before he moved again. Better to let the snipers think he might be dead or wounded than to leap up instantly and draw more fire. He reached down for his pistol, then thought better of it and moved slowly, cautiously, to fetch his driver's CETME rifle from the jeep without alerting any enemies that he was still alive.

It seemed to take forever, with the gunfire ringing out around him, but Ambika reached the weapon and withdrew it from the vehicle. If any hostiles had noticed him, they held their fire, reserving it for better targets near the trucks.

A glance downrange told Ambika his soldiers were dying. He saw four or five on the ground, either dead or unconscious. The others were firing at shadows, seemingly without direction, anything to stop the plunging fire that raked the trucks and second jeep.

Where was it coming from?

As if in answer to his silent question, the captain heard a short burst of automatic fire rattle away from the hillside directly opposite his position. Carefully, he wormed his way around the jeep and scanned the hill as best he could while lying half beneath it, peering out from below the rear bumper.

He saw a large man lean out from behind a boulder, aiming for perhaps a second, then unleashing several rounds from a Kalashnikov. The Russian rifle's sound was unmistakable to Ambika at such close range.

The captain wished his jeep had been the one outfitted with the heavy gun, but he could see the other, where it had crashed and stalled across the road. He knew he'd never get there if he tried running in the open toward the sniper's nest.

But he would do his best with what he had.

Ambika squirmed around, maintaining cover, while he sighted down the CETME's barrel toward the gunman's perch. It wasn't far away—less than a hundred feet, he guessed—but it would still require all of his skill and then some for a killing shot.

Don't try to kill him, then, Ambika thought. Just wound the man, or even pin him down until the others spot him and attack.

He could do that much, surely, even though he'd never shot a man before. Training had to count for something, or the army wouldn't bother with it, after all.

Ambika waited, peering through his rifle's sights with one eye closed, the other blinking in an effort to stay clear of salty, stinging sweat. His eye burned, fading in and out of focus, but the captain dared not wipe it, fearing he would miss his shot or rub sand into his eye from filthy hands. Instead, he mouthed a string of muttered curses, then bit hard upon his lower lip.

Come on, you bastard. Show yourself!

A blur of movement filled his sights, and he was firing, pouring half a magazine across the roadway toward the boulder and its rift where death lay waiting for his men. His rifle spewed out shiny cartridges, each one rebounding from the undercarriage of the jeep and piling up around him in the dirt.

When he released the trigger, staring hard across the road with both eyes open, Ambika saw nothing to indicate that he had struck his target. Had it merely been a shadow, or had he been lucky, taking down the sniper with a burst that slammed his body out of sight?

A worm of panic wriggled in his stomach, as he realized that there was only one way to find out. His soldiers seemed oblivious, still firing willy-nilly at the hillsides all around them, and he couldn't call them without standing up and waving.

If he had to be a target, Ambika decided, he would rather be a target on the move, attacking, carrying the battle to his foe.

But were there others? Could a single sniper have inflicted so much damage in so little time?

Ambika craned his neck, risking a head shot, and saw no one moving on the hills or in the roadside gullies. With so many of his soldiers firing, he could not pick out the sounds of any other weapons at the moment. It was down to him, a choice of risking everything or staying where he was.

Ambika lunged from cover, running hard across the road. He clutched the CETME rifle to his chest, ready to fire, praying with every step that he would find his enemy already dead.

12

Bolan waited for the rush he knew was coming, without being certain of how long he'd have to wait. One of the soldiers from the first jeep had survived and spotted him, tried nailing him and missed, but it had been a near-miss, with a couple of the bullets passing close enough for him to feel their hot breath on his skin.

Waiting was dangerous. His other enemies downrange regrouped and huddled to decide what they should do. If they got up the nerve to charge him all at once, behind a full screen of suppressing fire, Bolan knew it was doubtful that he would survive.

And so he waited, sweating, with the numbers running in his mind. The random firing from below meant that he wouldn't hear the enemy advancing, but would have to keep a watch. Another risk, but unavoidable.

He shifted slightly, eyeballing the gap beside the granite boulder. Seconds later, a lone soldier burst from cover near the jeep, charging across the road toward Bolan's roost. He held an automatic rifle, but he wasn't firing yet, and none of the collected soldiers near the two stalled trucks were offering support.

It could be now or never taking him, the Executioner decided, rolling even as the thought took shape to find his mark and make the shot. The running soldier saw enough of

Bolan to guess at what was coming. He leveled his autorifle from the hip, firing as he ran, without a break in stride.

Too late.

Bolan had target acquisition by that time, squeezed off a burst, ignored the swarm of angry hornets buzzing overhead. He saw his bullets strike the runner, jolt him like a carpet beaten on a clothesline. Bolan watched him stagger backward, going down, still firing as he fell.

And it was done.

He turned back toward the soldiers huddled by the trucks, in time to see one of them fall, shot in the back. That had to be Pahlavi, chipping in as best he could with nothing but a side arm. Bolan regretted that he hadn't snagged a rifle for his guide after their last engagement with the enemy, and vowed to remedy that failure.

If they both came out of it alive.

He shifted toward the trucks, drawing some concentrated fire this time. The one-man banzai charge had served a purpose for the enemy, giving the soldiers focus on Bolan's roost, and as more riflemen joined in the fusillade, he knew that a second rush would not be long in coming.

Thinking fast, he emptied his magazine to let them know exactly where he was, then swapped it for a fresh one as he moved, backtracking down the roadside to a secondary roost he'd picked out on arrival at the scene. The new nest didn't offer quite as much security, but if he played his cards right, by the time his adversaries knew that he had moved, it would already be too late.

The warrior crouched and waited, using the time that remained to unclip three Russian frag grenades and line them up for easy pitching when he needed them. There'd be no time for fumbling while his enemies advanced, and Bolan knew his life was hanging in the balance if he dropped the ball—or a grenade.

There was no time for him to spot Pahlavi, no way to communicate with his companion. That would also need a remedy, if they emerged victorious and he could find some kind of walkie-talkies on the battlefield. But for the moment, Bolan wasn't thinking much beyond the charge and how he would survive it, if he could.

The rush came suddenly, as suicidal charges had to, with the participants all screwing up their nerve at once and howling on the run, firing without much hope of hitting anything or anyone, a gesture and a vain attempt to sweep the field without incurring losses.

Bolan risked a glance onto the field and gauged his distance, primed and pitched the first grenade. While it was in the air, he pulled the second's pin and launched the bomb on a subtly different arc, to fall a few yards farther than the first. The third was armed and he was ready for the pitch when number one exploded, shattering the dusk with heavy-metal thunder and a swarm of anguished screams.

He made the final pitch, lay back in cover while the last two frag grenades went off, then came up firing from the gully. Bolan didn't try to count the soldiers who were down, already dead or dying on the field. Some of them might be stunned, without real injuries, but he would deal with that problem in time, as he was able.

Those still on their feet seemed dazed, disoriented, ducking in and out of drifting smoke clouds from the triple blasts, some firing off toward their original objective, while a number of the others hesitated, looking for another mark and wondering if they had been deceived. The answer to that question came as Bolan's bullets found them, short bursts reaching out to drop them, and from somewhere in their rear, the stubborn yapping of a Model 92 Beretta challenging the stragglers.

It was butchery, but Bolan didn't flinch from it, reloading when he'd used another magazine and fighting on, ducking the few rounds fired in his direction, answering with shots that silenced first one shooter, then another and another.

And somewhere in the midst of it, he knew that he would live to fight another day.

"DON'T SHOOT!" Pahlavi called out from the far side of the smoky killing ground. "It's only me!"

"Come on ahead," Bolan replied. "Pick up a rifle and some extra ammunition, while you're at it."

"From the dead?" Pahlavi asked nervously.

"Unless you find a stockpile in the trucks," Bolan replied, "I'd say it's your best bet."

"All right," the young man answered. "Yes, I'll find another weapon. You are right."

Moving among his fallen enemies, dispensing mercy here and there, Bolan called out, "I haven't seen the hostage from your village yet."

Pahlavi, with a captured CETME rifle slung across his shoulder, hesitated in the act of tugging at a dead man's bandolier. "He isn't on the field," he said. "I'll check the trucks."

"Be careful, just in case," Bolan advised.

Pahlavi walked around behind the first truck, leading with his liberated rifle as he peered across the tailgate, then stepped back and shook his head.

"No one," he said.

That still left one, and Bolan hoped they hadn't killed the prisoner they'd come to rescue—or provoked his captors into killing him at the beginning of their skirmish. It had always been a risk, but Bolan felt there'd been enough death for one afternoon, without another human sacrifice.

Pahlavi crept up to the second truck and repeated his technique of lunging for a look inside. This time, he scrambled higher up and waved to Bolan, shouting, "Here! I've found him. It's Jalil Yamuna."

Bolan recognized the name from conversation back in Giri, as they were preparing to depart. He didn't know the villager from Adam, but he didn't want the man to die. Accordingly, he rushed to join Pahlavi in the open truck, sweeping the field for any stray survivors as he closed the gap.

When Bolan reached the truck, Pahlavi was already slicing through the ropes that held the captive's hands behind his back. A moment later, busy with his folding knife, Pahlavi freed the stranger's legs, then stepped back while the man rose to his feet.

The liberated captive stared at Bolan for a moment, none too happily, then started speaking swiftly to his fellow countryman. Pahlavi listened for a moment, then translated.

"He was taken, as we know, for the possession of a rifle. They planned to interrogate him about me and the resistance, but he knows nothing to tell them. Now, he says, if more soldiers return, our people will be slaughtered."

"They should think about a change of scene," Bolan replied.

"Their lives are in the village," Pahlavi replied. "Most of them know nothing else."

"I take it they can learn, if they're alive," Bolan replied. "It's their choice, either way. If trouble's coming, they can either stand and face it, or move on."

"It's all my fault, you see?" Pahlavi cried out.

Bolan had no time for self-pity.

"What I see," he said, "is that someone spilled your name before you reached the village. If it was your sister or someone else, there's nothing we can do about it now. The troops were on their way to look for you before we got there, and they would've found this guy's Kalashnikov, regardless. Now, you've got a choice to make. Press on, or call it quits and try forgetting about Project X."

"There is no choice," Pahlavi said. "I cannot let their plans proceed."

"Then let's get on with business," Bolan said, "and knock off wasting time."

13

Cyrus Shabou lit his sixth cigarette of the day—the private limit he had set himself to test his discipline—and sent a stream of mentholated smoke wafting toward his office ceiling. Seated across the desk, Dr. Jamsheed Mehran endeavored not to let his disapproval show.

Shabou resolved to blow the rest of his smoke directly at Mehran to see how the scientist reacted. Meanwhile, he said, "I have received more news. All bad."

"I see."

It irritated Shabou that Mehran would not come out and ask what he had learned. The scientist insisted on his little power games, even when he was obviously the subordinate.

Shabou took another drag from his cigarette, held it for a moment, then sent the smoke cloud rolling toward Mehran, across his desktop. The visitor squirmed but refrained from gasping or fanning the air in front of his face.

"Apparently," Shabou explained, "another group of soldiers has been ambushed. There are no survivors, if my information is correct. You may be interested to know that this patrol had been dispatched to Giri."

"I see."

"You recognize the name, of course," Shabou said, unable to conceal his irritation at Mehran's calm.

"Giri? If I recall…that is—"

"How quickly we forget, Doctor." Shabou took pleasure in the scientist's discomfiture. "Giri. The native village of your traitor—and her brother. Are you with me, now?"

"Of course, sir. I remember it. And did they find him?"

"Therein lies the problem, I'm afraid," Shabou replied. "The officer in charge was sent to search the village for this Darius Pahlavi. Based on the location of the vehicles when found, it seems the soldiers were *returning* from their mission, but the officer did not communicate with his superiors. Therefore, they cannot tell if he had captured prisoners, or if the effort was in vain. Considering its outcome, though, I feel it's safe to say he touched a nerve."

"Yes, sir."

"You understand my difficulty, eh, Doctor?"

"Of course," Mehran replied, then caught himself. "That is, I mean to say—"

"If Project X is going to succeed, it must not be exposed to public scrutiny. These massacres, of course, define the very essence of sensational publicity. The army may be able to suppress reportage for a short time, but we can't depend on them. Since rural peasants found the bodies in both cases, word is bound to spread. And it will ultimately leak despite the best efforts of our compatriots in uniform."

"Yes, sir. I see that."

"Then you also see, my friend, why time is of the essence. If we're going to succeed *before* the project is exposed and global condemnation falls upon our heads, then we—I should say, *you*—are running out of time."

"You understand, Deputy Minister, that we have worked

around the clock to reach our goal, and I believe that we are very close."

"How close?" Shabou demanded.

"Well…in the realm of science, sir, precise predictions of that nature are… I mean to say…impossible."

Shabou said nothing. He preferred to let the grim expression on his face speak for him, leaving Mehran in no doubt as to his disappointment.

"But," the scientist hastened to add, "if we redouble our efforts, I'm fairly confident that we should have results within…three weeks?"

"Is that a question?" Shabou asked.

"No, sir. Three weeks."

"You'll stake your job on that? Your reputation? *Everything?*"

Dr. Mehran considered it, then swallowed hard and nodded. "Yes, sir. Yes, I will."

"So be it, then. But what if it should happen that we do not have three weeks? Suppose these rebels—Ohm, or whatever they call themselves today—should manage to go public in the meantime? Worse, suppose they raid the very laboratory?"

"Sir, we have advanced security in place."

"And so, presumably, do the armed forces," Shabou answered. "Yet they've lost the better part of eighty men today, from what I understand. Perhaps your chief of plant security should have another word with army headquarters."

"I'll tell him, sir, as soon as I leave here."

"And if a breach of your security occurs, by any chance, I trust there are procedures to contain it?" Shabou asked. "Some mechanism to preserve deniability?"

"If necessary, sir, we can destroy the plant and everything inside it."

"Would it seem to be an accident?"

Mehran nodded. "From the beginning, that was our intention."

"Like Chernobyl?"

"Heavens, no! We don't have a reactor, sir. We are not generating power. We have limited supplies of weapons-grade plutonium on hand, from which to build the devices."

"When you say it that way, it appears to be a simple thing," Shabou observed.

"Not *simple,* sir. I wouldn't go that far. The problem, as I've mentioned previously, is reduction of components. The materials involved are often delicate, and measurements must be precise. In essence, we are *shrinking* what has always been a large device, to make it portable by one man—and presumably an average man, at that—without reducing its impact substantially."

"I understand the goal, Doctor. You may recall that it was *I* who came to *you* for its accomplishment."

"Of course, Deputy Minister. I did not mean to indicate that—"

"What I'm curious to know," Shabou said, "is how you can fix a deadline for your research now, when problems still remain? And if you know today that three weeks is sufficient for completion of your task, could it not be completed within *two* weeks, for example?"

"Two weeks, sir?"

"Simply a question. Hypothetically."

"Well, hypothetically…"

"Two weeks would obviously give the traitors in our midst less time to sabotage the project and destroy all you have worked for through the past year and a half."

"Yes, sir. But—"

"Shall we say two weeks, then, as the final deadline? Have

you that much confidence in your own leadership and in the team you've chosen?"

"Sir—"

"Perfect. It's settled, then. Two weeks until we toast the ultimate success of Project X—or I find someone else to take your place."

Mehran was ashen-faced, but he could only nod in agreement. There was no room for debate in Shabou's tone or attitude.

"I should inform my team," Mehran replied, "without further delay. The deadline will mean extra shifts, of course, and no doubt some increased expense."

Shabou expelled another cloud of fragrant smoke and waved a broad hand through it, putting on his most expansive smile.

"Expense is not an issue, Doctor. And I'm sure your team will do its utmost to support you in this challenge. When the task is done, there will be time enough for them to rest."

In fact, Shabou already had a resting place in mind, where none of them would ever speak again of Project X—or anything at all.

"By all means, go and join your people. Use your expertise to the utmost. I trust that you won't let me down."

"No, sir," Mehran said quietly.

"That's excellent. Dismissed."

"TWO WEEKS?"

Dr. Simrin Amira gaped at Mehran in amazement. She could not have been more stunned if her superior had told her that he came from Jupiter. In fact, she might have been relieved in that case, since it would've indicated that Mehran had lost his mind.

Instead, Mehran just shrugged. "Two weeks," he said again. "Deputy Minister Shabou has ordered it."

"Oh, well. If he has *ordered* it, it must be possible. Is that your argument?"

"I have no argument," Mehran replied. "Just orders."

"To perform a task that's physically impossible!"

"I'm not convinced of that."

Amira frowned. "Since when?"

She watched Mehran stiffen, preparing to defend himself, and wished he had as much backbone when dealing with his superiors.

"Deputy Minister Shabou explained the urgency in no uncertain terms. With soldiers being killed in such large numbers, there is clearly danger of a breach in our security," Mehran explained.

"Danger from outside sources doesn't mean we can defy the laws of physics," Amira said. "If we rush—"

"Please, if I may," Kurush Gazsi said. "Dr. Mehran, you need have no concerns about security. I can assure you that—"

"It isn't me you must convince," Mehran said, cutting through the spiel. "Those who decide these things have had their say. We can obey or be replaced. And I assure you, when that happens, it will not be with a pension plan."

"'Those who decide these things'?" Amira echoed, mocking him. "There's no *decision* in this matter. It is not a test of willpower, whichever politician thinks he has a point to prove. We deal with science, in the realm of possibilities. If we are physically incapable of doing something, it means nothing to have a politician shouting, 'Finish it by Tuesday!'"

Mehran examined her as if a second head had sprouted from her shoulders. It was not his customary look. This new look had a cutting edge to it. It could draw blood, Amira guessed.

"I've never questioned your commitment to this project," he remarked, "until this moment."

"What?"

"Of course, if you're unwilling to proceed—"

"I have said nothing of the kind!" Amira exclaimed.

He forged ahead. "If you are unwilling to proceed within the guidelines we've been given from above, then I'm afraid you must resign."

"Resign!" Amira was shocked.

"Of course, your choice will be communicated to the ministry. Whatever action they deem necessary would proceed from there. I can't control that aspect of the matter, as I'm sure you understand."

Amira glanced at Gazsi, furious to find him smirking at her.

"I will *not* resign," she snapped. "I'm simply trying to communicate a fact that you, of all people, must recognize. Orders do not dictate the pace of scientific progress. It's a physical impossibility."

"Then we must work a miracle and *make* it possible," Mehran replied, straight-faced. The only change in his expression was a flare of angry color in his cheeks.

"I understand," Amira said at last.

"So, we're in full agreement?"

"As you say, Doctor."

"What will it take, then, to prepare a working model of the weapon in the time allotted?"

She had no idea, but couldn't say so. Any further opposition to the madness would surely see her fired from Project X, and likely sent directly to a prison cell, unless she "disappeared" somewhere along the way.

"More money," she responded. "Work around the clock."

"All possible," Mehran stated.

"And luck," she added. "I would say a great deal of good luck."

"I can't control that," Mehran answered, "but the money and

the personnel are guaranteed. Deputy Minister Shabou assured me of his full cooperation."

"Well, in that case, we should have no difficulties," Amira said.

"Sarcasm does not become you," Mehran chided her.

"Sarcasm, sir? I was agreeing with your judgment and the minister's."

Mehran leaned forward, planting bony elbows on his desk. "It may be difficult to meet our goal without an absolute commitment of the heart and mind," he said, speaking to Amira and Gazsi in turn. "We all must do our part in full, hold nothing back. I hope that's understood."

"Of course, Doctor," Gazsi said with an oily smile.

"I understand," Amira said.

"Let's make it happen, then. As for security, Kurush, while I appreciate your confidence, it has occurred to me that the rebels who've killed seventy or eighty soldiers in the past few hours may not find your team a great impediment if they decide to raid the lab."

Amira waited for the lab's chief of security to argue, but instead he simply said, "I will happily employ more personnel if funds are made available. As you're aware, Doctor, our budget—"

"I was thinking in a different vein," Mehran cut in. "Deputy Minister Shabou suggested that we seek help from the military. More specifically—"

"But, sir—"

"Specifically, that you consult Colonel Dalal and ask for help securing the lab. He is our nation's counterterrorism expert, after all, with more men and equipment at his fingertips than we can possibly afford. As for their training, well, you must agree that it surpasses anything the private sector can supply."

"In fact, sir—" Gazsi sputtered.

"Good. It's settled, then. I'm glad that you agree. I took the liberty of booking an appointment for you with the colonel. He's expecting you in—" Mehran checked his watch "—exactly thirty-two minutes. You'd best be on your way."

Flustered and fuming, Gazsi rose and hurried from the office without any parting pleasantries. His anger almost made Amira smile.

Almost.

Until she thought about the task ahead of her, and what awaited her if she should fail, as fail she would.

"Jamsheed," she said, "for heaven's sake. *Two weeks?*"

He shrugged. "What choice have we, Simrin? Of course, we can stand firm and tell them it's impossible. In which case, we'll be shot or thrown in prison, and the project will proceed with someone else in charge."

"And when *they* fail?" she challenged.

"We'll be vindicated from the grave. Does that please you?"

"They'll kill us anyway, Jamsheed, if we don't meet the deadline you've accepted."

"Then we'll meet it," he assured her. "One way or another, we shall meet it."

"It's impossible," she warned him for the last time.

Leaving Mehran's office, Amira had already turned her mind to methods of escape. She could go home to change her clothes, pick up her passport, never mind packing a bag. Before the lab staff missed her, she could be halfway to—

Standing in the corridor, a female uniformed security officer nodded to her, falling into step beside her. "I have been assigned to your protection, Doctor," she explained. "Director Gazsi is concerned that you may be at risk."

I'm sure he is, Amira thought, and forced a smile. "How generous of Mr. Gazsi."

"Not at all, Doctor," the officer replied. "From now until the project is completed, double the number of guards."

Simrin Amira read her doom in the young woman's round, bland face, and felt her final fleeting hope evaporate like water poured into a tub of sand.

Two weeks, she thought.

It didn't seem like much of a lifetime, at all.

14

Colonel Dalal was standing at his desk when Gazsi stepped into his office, following the officer who served as Dalal's secretary and receptionist. The colonel offered nothing in the way of salutation, simply waved his aide out of the room and waited for the door to close behind him as he left. Gazsi felt like an insect in a jar, being examined by a captor who had not decided whether he should be dissected or released.

"You've come at a bad time," Dalal said finally.

"I understand, sir. My request to see you was commanded by Deputy Minister Shabou and Dr. Jamsheed Mehran. If you would prefer that I not stay—"

"Sit down!" the colonel ordered gruffly. "I have no time at the moment for dramatics or for backroom politics."

As Gazsi settled on a straight, uncomfortable chair, Dalal asked him, "You've heard about the latest incident?"

"Yes, sir. A tragedy. For you to lose so many men—"

"Men and equipment," Dalal said, correcting him. "So far, seventy-nine men, three jeeps and two trucks damaged or destroyed. It's curious about the weapons, though, I grant you."

"Curious in what sense, sir?"

"That they were left behind, of course." Dalal dropped back

into his seat behind the desk, glaring. "You said you knew about these incidents."

"In general, that is. I mean to say—"

"Bandits or rebels should have made off with the guns and ammunition," Dalal said, forging ahead. "Would they leave nearly eighty rifles on the field, with handguns and a heavy machine gun? Ridiculous!"

"If I may ask, sir, in that case…what is your theory?"

"Theory?" The very word appeared to irritate Dalal. "I'm not employed to *theorize.* I deal in facts. My men were killed, their weapons left behind. Therefore, the men who killed them have no need of weapons. They are well prepared."

"Perhaps a small group," Gazsi offered. "Very small, in fact, with no real growth potential."

"Small? How small?" Dalal demanded.

"I would just be theorizing, Colonel."

"Then, by all means, do so!"

"As you're well aware, there is apparently a small but dedicated group of individuals committed to disrupting Dr. Mehran's project."

"Ohm?" Dalal replied. "The academics?"

"I believe—and, may I add, Deputy Minister Shabou appears to share my feelings in this matter—that we may have underestimated their potential for disruption. Since the woman was discovered—"

"In your laboratory," Dalal said. "Under your very nose."

"Since then, I have been forced to reconsider my original judgment of Ohm and its members. This Darius Pahlavi, for example—"

"Oh, you want to talk about Pahlavi?" Dalal interrupted. "The last group of soldiers I lost were assigned to retrieve him. Or, rather, to frighten his friends and relatives until they betrayed him. The captain, it seems, was a negligent fool. I may have to award him a medal, to whitewash his failure."

"Colonel—"

"And now, I suppose, you want more of my soldiers to help do your job for you?"

"Sir, I am here, as I said—"

"On the orders of others. I know." Dalal sneered. "If it weren't for those others, you'd never get past the front gate. May I tell you something, in confidence? Just between us?"

Stiffly, Gazsi replied, "Of course, Colonel."

"I don't trust private spies or meddlers in security. You're all alike to me, in it for profit first, and never mind who wins, as long as you get paid. I hold you and your kind in absolute contempt. That said, you've found a niche where you're protected—for the moment—by some influential men. Beware of what may happen with that influence removed."

"Surely you don't suggest removing Minister Shabou?"

"Deputy Minister," Dalal corrected him, "and I've suggested no such thing, as you well know. The tape and transcript of our conversation will support me."

"Naturally. Colonel, may we discuss the purpose of my visit? Since it pains you so, I wish to keep it brief."

"We've been discussing it," Dalal replied. "You've come to seek more men, more guns, more something I can ill afford to lose, with soldiers dying all around me. And you likely have authority to issue the request as a demand."

"I do, in fact," Gazsi said. "Yes, sir."

"Tell me, then, and we shall see if what you wish is even possible."

"Another fifty men to guard the laboratory for the next two weeks. I'm told a breakthrough is expected then, but in the meantime, it is critical to keep out all disruptive elements."

"Fifty? Why not two hundred? I can always go before the General Staff and tell them their allotment for our district is inadequate, because a scientist needs men to babysit his employees."

"I have good reason to believe the General Staff is well aware of Project X," Gazsi replied. "But if you feel the need to tell them, sir, I obviously have no power to prevent you," Gazsi said with a slight smile.

Colonel Dalal considered that. "Not yet," he said. "You ask for fifty men. I shall provide them. When the next attack comes—and I have no doubt that there will be another—if I find myself shorthanded, *then* I will inform the General Staff precisely why I cannot execute my duties as expected. I will leave them in no doubt as to responsibility."

"With luck and Allah's grace, Colonel, no such report will be required. I hope, with Dr. Mehran and the others, that their work may be successful. If it is, you'll find that Project X eliminates whatever small concerns you feel today, regarding your superiors."

"It's my *inferiors* that trouble me," Dalal answered. "They try to rise above their place, and thus unbalance everything."

"It is the nature of humanity," Gazsi replied.

"Humanity?" For the first time in Gazsi's personal experience, the colonel smiled. "Were *you* humane, Gazsi? With your young traitor? With the woman? Did you show her your humanity?"

Gazsi remained impassive, would not let himself be baited.

"In the circumstances," he replied, "I'd say I was extremely generous."

DARICE PAHLAVI WASN'T sure how long she had been kept in darkness, but she knew it had to have been days, at least. Not weeks—it didn't feel that long—but time was meaningless when total deprivation of the senses was imposed.

That wasn't strictly true, of course. Her cell was blacker than the bottom of a coal mine, but her other senses were intact. She heard the drip of water, sometimes, and the scurrying of unseen insects, which in turn raised goose bumps on her skin. She smelled the filth that they refused to clear out of her cell, along with mildew, dampened stone and the unpleasant odors of herself. She tasted perspiration on her upper lip, and twice a day the filthy gruel that passed for food.

Delivery of meals was the only time the darkness of her cell was broken. Then, after a muffled sound of footsteps from the corridor outside, a plate or hatch was opened near the bottom of her cell's iron door, light spilling briefly through it to illuminate a tin plate filled with goulash or stew or whatever it was called. It always tasted bland or bitter, and it never satisfied her hunger, but she ate it just the same.

They brought no water to her cell, but she had found a dripping spigot in a corner of the tiny room, and she could wet her tongue, one rusty-tasting droplet at a time. The bucket in another corner was her toilet. It had not been emptied yet, which told Darice her estimate of time was probably correct— or else, her jailers simply did not care.

That might be true, since they had ceased to question her. Soon after she was captured, Gazsi and his minions had been at her constantly, demanding information, names, addresses, explanations. They had broken her—no human being could endure such pain and still keep silent—but the rules of Ohm dictated that she had known little of the group itself. There was not much for her to share.

Except her brother's name, and the location of their native village. That was in her file, of course, all part of what she had disclosed to get her job with Project X, before she knew that it was evil. As for other names, she knew none, could not help her tormentors find others to abduct and torture.

That had angered them, increased her suffering, until they realized at last that she was keeping nothing from them. Darice had been on the verge of fabricating things, drawing fictitious characters from her imagination to relieve the pain, and in the hope that when Gazsi discovered she was lying, he'd be furious enough to grant her the release of death.

But she was still living, still entombed.

Darice had no idea why they were keeping her alive. By any common definition of the term, she was a traitor to her country—or, at least, to those who wished to sacrifice it for a fleeting dream of glory etched in fire and fallout. It made better sense to kill her than to keep her caged, in case their plan fell through and she was found by someone else, compelled to testify against the men and women who controlled the nightmare known as Project X.

Still, she supposed there would be time enough to dispose of her if the tide turned against them. If they were successful, if the weapon was completed and they sent it out into the field, nothing Darice could say would matter. She could not call the bombers home, turn back the calendar, erase the catastrophic damage that was done.

She knew no magic, could not work a miracle.

But her brother, if he was still alive, might find a way to stop the worst of it. She trusted him, without even the vaguest of ideas how he'd accomplish such a thing. He was intelligent, courageous and had contacts in the outside world, although he wisely never shared the details of those links with her.

Would Allah help her brother, she wondered, or was He in league with the destroyers, as so many of the ultra-fundamentalists proclaimed? If so, their cause was lost and she was on the wrong side of it, anyway, fighting against the will of Allah.

But Darice didn't believe that.

Allah, by whatever name his human followers might call him, was supposed to be all-powerful. He did not need a weapon in a suitcase to destroy the world, if that was His intent. He could send famine, floods, earthquakes—most anything, to purge the Earth of human life, if He so chose.

Allah did not need Project X.

Darice knew that was the brainchild of demented human beings who would rather sacrifice their nation, and perhaps their very race, than live in peace with those whose politics and personal beliefs were slightly different. Because they were insane, willing to slaughter millions in pursuit of their own warped agenda, they thought nothing of a simple lie, claiming that Allah had endorsed their scheme. She knew simple believers—sometimes mentally unbalanced, often raised from infancy to trust their "betters"—took the lies as truth and offered no objection.

When they knew about the master plan at all.

Deception was another part of Project X that told Darice it was a fraud. She understood the need for secrecy in politics and national defense, but this was different. The project had no benign aspects, served no one but a handful of conspirators who risked the end of human history to write its final page themselves.

If there was something more Darice could do to stop them, she would gladly sacrifice herself and—

She heard footsteps in the corridor.

She didn't think that it was feeding time. That could be a mistake, of course, but she would simply have to wait and see. There might be other cells along the corridor, but when she stretched her mind back to her first day of captivity, she could not recall footsteps coming for anyone but her.

She counted off some thirty seconds in her head, then heard a key scrape in the lock of her cell's door. It opened with a flood of light that stabbed into her eyes and made her close them, grimacing against the sudden pain.

Several men entered, and she recognized Kurush Gazsi's cheap aftershave lotion before her eyes swam into focus, picking out his form flanked by a pair of guards.

"Darice," he said, "we've come to speak with you."

"I have nothing to tell you," she replied. "You already know everything."

Gazsi chuckled. "If only it were true," he said, "my job would be a great deal easier. Unfortunately, you're mistaken. I have much to learn, and you will help me."

"No," Darice said plainly.

"Oh, yes," he said with chilling confidence. "You may not know it yet, but you're my secret weapon."

"What, another one?" she asked.

"For now," Gazsi replied, "the only one I need."

15

Pahlavi gave Bolan directions to their target, the home of Project X. The Pakistani was convinced that they couldn't crack the lab compound alone, and so—despite Bolan's objections to the contrary—they were proceeding instead to meet the members of Ohm.

The Executioner wasn't sure what to expect from the group, and Pahlavi was playing it close to the vest, keeping the names and profiles to himself. Perhaps it was a sense of loyalty, or fear that Bolan might be captured and interrogated, but it hardly mattered at the moment. Even if he praised his comrades in effusive terms, the Executioner could only judge them when they stood before him in the flesh, when he could gauge their willingness to fight.

As for their skill, Bolan wasn't expecting too much.

Pahlavi's first two helpers, Adi and Sanjiv, had both shown courage on the firing line, but raw guts hadn't been enough to get them through it. Both were dead now, and while Bolan shouldered no responsibility for that, he hoped he wouldn't leave more friendly ghosts behind him when he left this country.

He drove, Pahlavi navigating without maps, filling the gaps between directions with the story of his life. Near the beginning, Bolan had considered telling him to can it, but he thought maybe it helped the young man to detail his roots, his upbringing, and Bolan had a knack for tuning out small talk when it got in the way. He reckoned that Pahlavi's monologue was better than whatever unintelligible songs he would've gotten on the car's radio.

And it was good, sometimes, to know your allies, understand the burdens on their minds and hearts that had propelled them from an ordinary life of nine-to-five conformity, into a course of action that could get them killed. No one in his or her right mind joined a revolution on a whim, at least when it was clear the rebels were the losing side. No normal person gave up home and family and future if there was another viable alternative.

Pahlavi and his friends in Ohm would share a sense of mission. That was basic to resistance movements everywhere, but as history had amply demonstrated time and time again, some causes were not worth pursuing, even if their boosters were the most committed people in the world. In Ohm's case, Bolan happened to agree that stopping World War III was a worthy cause—if he could pull it off.

As for the help Ohm could provide, beyond directions to the front and briefings on his opposition, that remained for Bolan to discover when he met the other players. If he sized them up as people who could do the job—or give it their best shot, in any case—he would construct a plan incorporating them in whatever capacity he deemed appropriate.

That didn't mean that all of them would wind up being front-line fighters. In the Executioner's experience, a willingness to die wasn't the same thing as ability to fight, to kill, or even to make dying count for something on the battlefield. Any moron could throw himself beneath a speeding tank or walk around exposed to sniper fire until a bullet took him down. For all the good it did their side, those "soldiers" may as well have stayed home in the first place, left the fighting to the ones who knew that dying was a risk but didn't court it like a long-lost lover.

Every morning of his life, Mack Bolan thanked the Universe that he was still alive and fit for duty. When his time came, he would meet the rush head-on and take it like a man. But in the meantime, he had no interest in teaming up with suicidal dilettantes who thought that dying for their cause was the primary goal of waging war.

"We have another thirty minutes, I believe," Pahlavi said, cutting into Bolan's thoughts. "I'll tell you where to turn."

"These friends of yours," Bolan said. "Are they like you, or is it more an ivory-tower thing for them?"

Pahlavi paused to weigh the compliment, seemed pleased that Bolan saw him as a soldier, even if an inexperienced and amateur one.

"They are like me," he said at last. "All have lost loved ones to the prisons, the interrogation rooms, the firing squads. Most are young. Only a few of them have children, but they don't want crazy people to destroy the world."

"And what about experience? Are any of them former soldiers?"

"Two or three," Pahlavi said. "Not many. We have no conscription here in Pakistan, although the law of 1952 permits it. Volunteers may join the army at sixteen and fight at eighteen years of age. So far, the volunteer rate has been adequate, but most of those who have complaints against the government do not enlist."

Okay, Bolan thought. Two or three trained fighters in a group composed of earnest wannabes. That didn't mean some of the others couldn't shoot or fight, but he would have to check them out himself.

"How many friends are you expecting?" he inquired.

"Thirty were summoned. I can't say how many will respond," Pahlavi answered.

"What about equipment?"

"We have weapons," his guide said. "Don't worry about that. If you had not arrived, we were prepared to do this by ourselves."

"You may be willing," Bolan said. "We'll have to wait and see if you're prepared."

"You won't be disappointed," Pahlavi said.

Bolan drove on through the night in silence, hoping that his guide was right.

A CHANCE ENCOUNTER had led Manoj Shankara to the move that changed his life forever. He had never dreamed himself a hero, never thought he would do anything extraordinary, but sometimes an ordinary man in extraordinary circumstances could surprise himself.

It was Darice Pahlavi's fault, of course. If she had not befriended him, if she had left him to admire her beauty from afar, Shankara likely would've managed to ignore the comment he overheard in passing from Kurush Gazsi, the chief of plant security. Indeed, if Darice had not introduced him to the concept of freethinking and resistance to misguided power, then Shankara thought he probably would have accepted the reports that she had left the job to wed a childhood sweetheart, or the rumors that she'd quarreled with a supervisor and was fired.

But he knew those were lies.

To start with, there had been no lover. He was certain Darice would have mentioned one at some point in their conversations, and Shankara would have filed the name away, hating the man who touched what he could only worship in silence.

As for an argument, Darice was capable of flare-ups, but there had been none the day she disappeared, or for at least two weeks beforehand. And she *never* talked back to superiors around the lab. It would have been unthinkable.

Aside from his analysis of Darice and her character, Shankara knew the stories told around the lab were lies because Darice had warned him in advance that something bad might happen to her. On the very day she disappeared, she'd taken him aside and whispered urgently, "If anything goes wrong, please warn my brother. You know Darius?"

Shankara had met Darius Pahlavi twice, at weekend outings organized for members of the lab team and their families. Darius shook his hand but frowned at him, as if he recognized the lust that simmered in Shankara's heart.

"Do not go to his home," Darice had said, forgetting in her haste that Shankara had no clue where that might be. And then she'd given him directions to a small house in the country where her brother could be contacted in the event of an emergency. She'd thanked him, kissed him lightly on the cheek and turned away.

The next morning, the lab was informed she was gone.

Shankara had done nothing. He was not a hero, didn't fully understand the politics or import of some of the things Darice had told him. If he was honest with himself, there had been times when he was frightened of his own shadow, but the bright lights of the laboratory kept all that at bay. Shankara had a gift in that department, was respected there—at least, for his abilities—and did not plan to throw it all away.

Darice, he'd told himself, had meddled in some things bes

left alone. There was no real doubt in his mind that she'd betrayed the project somehow and had paid the final price. Shankara could not raise her from the dead, and frankly didn't care enough about her brother to risk death himself, just for warning Darius.

All that had changed within a few brief seconds, though, thanks to curry and coincidence. The curry was Shankara's breakfast, and it sent him bustling to the men's room midway through his morning shift. He had been huddled in a stall when two men entered, minutes after him, and he'd recognized Gazsi's voice.

"No, it doesn't matter any longer if the bitch can't tell us anything," Gazsi said. "We can still use her as bait."

"I'm not sure that will work, sir," the second man said. One of the guards, perhaps.

"Well, *I'm* sure," Gazsi answered with his trademark arrogance. "She'll draw the brother like a fly to shit, and when we have him, we'll soon have the rest of Ohm."

Shankara had already raised his feet to keep them out of sight beneath the half door of his toilet stall. Gazsi and his unknown companion finished urinating, washed their hands and left, while Shankara clenched his teeth and cheeks against a blast of flatulence that would reveal him as a spy.

When they were gone, he'd slumped into relief, mind racing to interpret what he'd heard. The "bitch," he took for granted, was Darice Pahlavi. No one else was missing from the lab, and it was evident from Gazsi's words that she had been interrogated. Also, mention of "the brother" cinched it in his mind. And Ohm—the symbol for resistance in his scientific world— was simply the icing on the cake.

Shankara took his time emerging from the men's room, giving Gazsi and his sidekick a decent lead. The walk back to his workstation was torment, with his mind and heart in turmoil simultaneously.

Darice was alive, that much was crystal clear. And she had suffered at the monster Gazsi's hands. Might still be suffering, for all Shankara knew.

But where was she?

He'd never find out for himself, and even if he did, what could he do about it? Charge in like a knight on a white steed and rescue her from armed security guards who were trained to disable and kill? It almost made him weep, the image in his mind was so pathetic. So inadequate.

He could not save her, but perhaps he *could* do what Darice had asked of him in friendship on the day she disappeared. He could do that, at least, and possibly in some small way relieve the agony of guilt he suffered for betraying her.

Or maybe there was no relief. Maybe he had to suffer for his sin of silence, even as he tried to make it right. Too little and too late, perhaps, but Shankara would try his best.

And he could not afford to wait.

If he delayed until his shift was over, Gazsi might have put some plan in motion that would trap Darice's brother and the rest. Logic told him the plan was already in place, the trap already baited, but he had to try.

And that meant getting out, despite the stringent new security precautions Gazsi had enacted, while Dr. Mehran had fixed a hopelessly unrealistic two-week deadline for completion of their work. Shankara had raised no objection, even knowing that the goal was unattainable. The lot of them would fail together, but he knew from past experience that squeaky wheels were sometimes greased in most unpleasant ways.

Now, it was time to flee, and curry might be his salvation. Stranger things had happened.

He approached Dr. Mehran, wearing a pained expression on his face, and waited for the great man to complete his scribblings on a clipboard.

Glancing up at last, Mehran asked, "What is it, Manoj?"

"With most sincere apologies, Doctor, I have, er, that is…something of a medical emergency."

16

The house stood out in the middle of nowhere, approached by a single-lane track that had never been paved. Bolan might have called it a farmhouse, but there was no farm in sight, just weed-choked fields with scattered trees, then forest rising up behind the house to shield it from north winds.

The place appeared to be deserted. Bolan couldn't tell how recently another vehicle had passed along the rutted access road, but there were no cars visible around the house or its dilapidated outbuildings. As they approached, rocking and rolling over potholes, Bolan saw that certain shingles from the roof had either fallen in or blown away, leaving rafters exposed.

"You're sure this is the place?" he asked Pahlavi.

"I am sure."

"Looks like we missed the party."

"They will be here."

Bolan heard the quiet certainty in his companion's tone, reckoned Pahlavi thought he was correct in any case, whether the other Ohm members showed or not.

The idea of an ambush by Pahlavi's people had never entered Bolan's mind. They'd come too far and done too much together for the Pakistani to prove false.

But what if someone else had learned about the rendezvous before they got there?

"Are your people solid?" Bolan asked.

"Solid?"

"Trustworthy. Is there any chance at all you have a mole inside the group?"

Pahlavi frowned and shook his head. "It is impossible. I stake my life on that."

"Friend, you already have," the Executioner replied grimly.

They closed the gap to fifty yards, then thirty. As they entered what would normally have been the house's yard, Bolan made out a flicker in the nearest window, as if someone passed quickly on the inside.

"There's company," Bolan said.

"Yes," Pahlavi said. "My friends."

And suddenly, they were surrounded. It was no great trick, considering the waist-high grass and weeds, but Bolan gave them points for avoiding the car as he'd pulled off the dirt track, closing in behind him while the bulk of his attention focused on the house.

It wasn't Special Forces good, by any means—but maybe it was good enough.

The people who had risen from the weeds around his car were all Pahlavi's age or younger, dressed in hiking clothes and heavy on the earth tones, going for the next best thing to camouflage. Befitting Pakistan, they had no dearth of weapons, every one of them holding some kind of automatic rifle, submachine gun, or police-style shotgun.

Bolan realized that they could take him now, if they were so inclined and didn't mind Pahlavi dying with him. If they opened fire in concert, they could strafe the car and kill both occupants—together with a few of their own number, since they hadn't calculated fields of crossfire and were begging for a deadly accident.

"They're on your side?" Bolan inquired.

"*Our* side," Pahlavi stressed. "You're one of us."

That said, he stepped out of the car and started greeting members of the ambush party, shaking hands and slapping backs, kissing a female cheek from time to time. Bolan unfolded from the driver's seat, keeping his hands in plain view all the time and making no moves toward the pistol in his shoulder rig.

The Ohm guerrillas on his side watched him, their weapons held discreetly angled toward the ground, with index fingers never far outside their trigger guards. So far, considering the fact that only two or three of them had any kind of military background, Bolan was impressed.

Pahlavi made the rounds, a full 360-degree circuit of the car, before he started in on introductions. Bolan listened carefully, repeating names aloud to match them permanently with the earnest faces in his mind. His mental mug file hadn't reached its limit yet, although he kept expecting that the next person he met would force him to delete one of the older dossiers he'd logged between his ears. When that day came, Bolan hoped he could start by weeding out the dead.

He counted nineteen faces, nineteen names. A twentieth was waiting for them on the porch of the old house, the youngest female out of seven in the group, and seemingly unarmed. Pahlavi kissed her on the lips, rather than on the cheek, and clutched her to his chest a moment longer than he would have done a simple friend.

That done, he turned to Bolan, beckoning. "Please, come inside with us. Pitri will hide the car."

SHANKARA HAD RETREATED to the men's room, fretting, after Dr. Mehran had refused to let him leave the complex. Mehran had been stern, referring to their deadline and the earlier announcement that they would be staying at the plant and working around-the-clock in shifts until their goal was met.

If Shankara felt unwell, Mehran reminded him, the plant had many toilets and a doctor constantly on call. The medic likely could dispense something to cure him within the hour, but no member of the staff would leave the complex short of mortal injury.

Shankara was polite, no storming off to draw further attention. He had played his only card and lost. It was the point where he would normally give up, follow the path of least resistance, but he could not bear the guilt already gnawing at him from within.

Darice had been his one friend at the plant, although he'd wanted so much more. Never expressed, his yearning for her tortured him, as Gazsi's goon squad had to have tortured her.

I must warn Darius! he thought. But how?

If Mehran would not let him go, Shankara knew he had to escape by other means. It would require a desperate effort, but he could not bear to live with the alternative.

First, he required a plan. That was the easy part, since theories and calculations comprised his life. He would prepare a dummy file and transport it by hand from Building C, the lab where he had worked for nineteen months, to the administration block in Building A. That would put him near the exits to the parking lot where he had left his car eight hours earlier, not knowing that he might not sit behind the wheel again for fourteen days.

There would be guards, of course. That part would call for unaccustomed courage on his part, but once he reached his car, Shankara only had to crash one checkpoint and a chain-link gate to reach the highway and escape.

Only.

It sounded simple in his mind, but he knew the reality was something else again.

He left the men's room, careful to first wash his trembling hands, and walked back to his workstation. Shankara had a whole box of manila folders there, although most work was filed on disks and on the hard drive of the plant's mainframe computers. Gathering a random stack of papers, several of them blank, Shankara squared them neatly, placed them in the folder and began his walk to Building A, praying that he would not meet Dr. Mehran on his way.

Nor did he, passing by the workstations of colleagues and the empty place once occupied by she whom he was bent on rescuing. The others barely glanced at him, absorbed by calculations and equations, test results, schematic drawings and the like. Shankara was not popular among his fellow workers, never had been. He supposed that none of them would miss him when he'd fled—or when the guards had murdered him.

He cleared the lab proper and reached the first checkpoint. A guard in uniform stood watching his approach, arms crossed, a submachine gun slung across one shoulder, pistol on his hip.

"Where are you going?" the guard asked.

"I have a file for Building A."

"Clearance?"

Here was the sticking point. "Apparently," Shankara said. "They called for it, just now."

The guard could check that easily enough. It would only take an in-house phone call, or a short chat on his two-way radio. In that case, Shankara thought, he would be as good as dead.

He wondered whether he would catch a last glimpse of Darice, as he passed by her holding cell en route to a blood-smeared torture chamber, or if Gazsi's men would merely shoot him on the spot.

"What's in the file?" the guard inquired.

Shankara stared at him, as if the man in uniform had grown a second head before his very eyes. "It's classified, of course," he answered stiffly.

"Hmph. All right, then. Go ahead," the guard replied.

Shankara nearly wilted with relief, then thought that it might be some kind of trick. The guard would let him walk a few more steps, then shoot him in the back. Police and soldiers sometimes did such things, or so he'd heard. Still, having once received the go-ahead, Shankara had no choice but to proceed.

He passed the guard with shoulder muscles clenched against the impact of a bullet, only let himself relax once he had cleared the building, moving freely through the open air toward Building A. It was a relatively short walk, only fifty yards or so, but in his mind it seemed to stretch for miles. Guards passed him on the way, staring into his eyes and at the folder in his hand, but none saw fit to challenge him.

He reached Administration, cleared the outer door and paused for just a beat, to get his bearings. Even though Shankara followed that same path five days a week, going and coming, to and from his work, it all seemed alien to him at the moment. He had to pause, locate the exit that he wanted, casually veering off in that direction. Taking one step at a time.

"Hold on, there!"

Turning toward the voice, off to his left, he saw another guard. This one was taller, somewhat older, with his chin cleft by an ancient scar. His stare felt like an X-ray, penetrating through Shankara's clothes and flesh to find the treachery inside his heart.

"Yes?" Shankara said. His voice cracked, as if he were on the verge of puberty.

"Where are you going?" the guard asked.

Shankara raised his folder like a shield. "I have a file for Building A," he said.

"For who in Building A?" the guard demanded to know.

Allah help me! Shankara thought.

"I don't know," Shankara answered, trembling where he stood. "A secretary called. Said to bring the file. My supervisor didn't give a name."

"Come over here," the guard commanded, "while I check on this."

Shankara did as he was told, stepped closer, fighting waves of sudden nausea as the guard half turned his head, angling his lips toward the radio microphone clipped to his left epaulette.

Shankara did not plan to drop the file. His fingers simply could not hold it any longer, let the folder slip between them, spilling its mismatched and pointless contents all around the guard's spit-polished boots.

The whimper of embarrassment escaping from Shankara's throat was genuine, as he bent to fetch the papers, but it changed almost at once into a snarl of rage, surprising him.

Instead of picking up the folder, Shankara found himself clenching both hands into fists, whipping one through a short arc into the guard's unprotected groin. He scored a hit, half-surprised when the guard doubled over in pain, still reaching instinctively for his holstered pistol.

Shankara rose, slamming his knee into the stranger's face. He didn't wait to see the guard go down, but rather turned and bolted for the exit and the parking lot that beckoned like salvation. He ran for his life, as somewhere in the depths of Building A, a siren blared.

BOLAN REVIEWED THE TROOPS, such as they were, while Pahlavi talked about the details of his plan. In essence, it involved approaching the stronghold of Project X in force and somehow getting past the outer fence, then dealing with the guards as they appeared and raising hell inside the lab to render it inoperable.

Bolan listened to the broad strokes, while he studied the assembled rebels and their arms. As he'd supposed, their weapons came from bootleg arms bazaars all over Pakistan, heavy on AK-47 variants and CETME autorifles, but including one Galil, a Belgian FNC, a Skorpion machine pistol and a pair of French MAT submachine guns. The rifles weren't a problem, when it came to ammunition, since most armies had converted to the standard NATO rounds, in 5.56 mm or 7.62 mm. The shotguns were 12-gauge pump-actions. Side arms were a motley collection, ranging from an old .38-caliber revolver with rust spots on its four-inch barrel to Browning Hi-Powers, a couple of Makarovs, and a surprise Desert Eagle chambered in .41 Magnum.

As for the "soldiers," Bolan had seen better—but he'd also seen much worse. They all seemed fit enough, no anorexics or candidates for heart failure from morbid obesity, none with any apparent disabilities. The grim determination in their faces told him they would fight—or that they meant to, anyway. He wouldn't really know, until he saw them on the firing line, if that was courage or a cool eleventh-hour bluff.

"I need to see a layout of the plant before we start," he told Pahlavi, when the Pakistani finished talking through his plan. "Draw it to scale, the best you can, including all the fences and security equipment you're aware of."

Smiling as he spoke, Pahlavi said, "It's done, already. Janna, please?"

Pahlavi's girlfriend from the porch produced a rolled-up tube of paper, stepped between them and began to spread it on an oblong table, using ashtrays, plastic glasses and a snubby automatic pistol to secure the corners. Homely paperweights, Bolan thought.

The drawing wasn't bad. Someone had spent a fair amount of time on it, perhaps with drafting tools, to get it right. They had proportions penciled in, giving the scale, with buildings labeled A through E—or so Bolan discovered, as Pahlavi translated the legends into English.

He began a walking tour, pointing to this or that in turn, describing fences, car parks, laboratories, an administration building, water towers, generators. It had everything a self-sufficient rural plant would need to operate in secrecy, without relying overmuch on nearby towns.

After the basics were detailed, Janna produced more drawings, and Pahlavi took them through the floor plans for each building one by one. For Bolan's benefit, he noted that his sister had supplied the basic sketches, which evolved with help from someone named Darshan—apparently a draftsman—into what they saw before them.

Bolan paid attention, asking questions when he needed to, if something wasn't clear. For the most part, it was a textbook-perfect briefing, down to educated guesswork on the personnel they'd have to deal with, if and when they breached the fence.

"You've done good work," Bolan said, when Pahlavi finished, "but you have to know it's dated, now. After today, there'll be enhanced security. Most likely, they'll increase the guard force. Look for army regulars, if they've got men to spare. It won't be easy, going in. Some of us probably won't make it."

No one answered that until Pahlavi said, "We are prepared."

"I hope so," the Executioner told them all. "Because the only rule from this point on is do-or-die."

17

Shankara thought it was a miracle that he was still alive, much less that he was free and racing down the highway toward his impulsive rendezvous with Darius Pahlavi. He would have preferred that Pahlavi knew he was coming, that he would be there to meet Shankara on arrival, but he only had an address and could not afford to stop to try to find the telephone number.

His strength was failing, and the blood would draw unwelcome notice.

There was pain, of course. Shankara had expected that, and almost welcomed it, since it kept him awake. Without the pain, he was convinced that he'd have slumped into unconsciousness by now and wrecked his car. It had already suffered damage, crashing through the compound's gates, but if he drove it off the road and mired it in sand or mud, Shankara knew he was as good as dead.

Don't kid yourself, he thought. You're dying now.

Perhaps. But if he was, there still might be sufficient time for him to warn Pahlavi and report that Darice was alive.

Perhaps.

Shankara had surprised himself, when he attacked the guard in Building A and sent him sprawling. It was all chaotic and a little blurry after that. The sprint to reach his car, as the alarms began to whoop and moan around him. Reaching it as more guards hustled from Administration, running after him. He'd somehow managed to outrun them, climb into his car and start the engine as they raced across the parking lot with guns drawn. And he'd crashed both gates as they began to fire at him, their bullets peppering the car and smashing out his rear window.

One of those shots, at least, had found its way into Shankara's back. He'd felt the impact, like a hard slap with an open hand, but thought perhaps the slug was just embedded in the padding of the driver's seat. It was the excitement of the chase, speeding along at better than 70 miles per hour, using back roads where he could and nearly getting lost in one town that he couldn't even name.

A full half hour after his escape Shankara felt the blood soaking through his shirt and running down inside the waistband of his slacks. On noting that, he'd reached behind himself and drawn back fingers streaked with crimson. Pain had followed the first sight of blood, and while he tried to take stock of his injuries—both lungs still functioning, his arms mobile, his heart still pumping fitfully—Shankara knew he couldn't last much longer without help.

But there was no help to be had, unless he reached his destination, told his story, begged Pahlavi to forgive him for not helping when Darice was taken from the lab.

If he stopped now, Shankara knew that there were only two alternatives. Blood loss might kill him where he sat, or his pursuers would discover him still living. He could not predict if they would finish him immediately or attempt to save him for interrogation, but since neither prospect offered any hope, he thought the best option was to forge ahead and try to pay his debt.

It couldn't be much farther, could it? He had lost all track of time, but there were landmarks that Darice had listed for him, and Shankara had already seen most of them, ticked them off in passing as a way to reassure himself that he was on the right track, wasn't lost and wasting the last moments he had left on Earth.

The house should be close. Granted, he was having problems with his vision, blurring in and out of focus while he drove, but there was no doubt in his mind that he could recognize a house on sight.

He only hoped that it would be *the* house.

Any mistake at this point would be fatal. If he stopped at the wrong place, got out and staggered to the door, he would exhaust his last reserve of strength for nothing. Strangers would recoil from him in horror, and would likely summon the authorities to cart him off for slaughter.

No. He had to get it right the first time. Drive directly to the house with trees around it and present himself to Darius Pahlavi. He would tell Darice's brother what he knew, and pray to Allah that he had not come too late.

Was that the house, on his left? It matched the physical description given to him by Darice, some time ago, but there was only one way to be sure. He had to take the risk, knowing that if he erred, his flight and sacrifice were wasted, all for nothing.

Grim-faced, grinding teeth against the pain, Shankara turned his bullet-punctured car into the narrow country lane and drove slowly toward the old, dilapidated house.

ONE OF THE FRONT PORCH sentries called out to Pahlavi, something urgent. Bolan saw his guide blink once and lift his rifle from the floor.

"A car is coming," Pahlavi said.

"And you're not expecting anyone?"

"There's no one else."

Bolan retrieved his AKMS from the duffel bag and moved

to join Pahlavi at the nearest window. What he saw, approaching without stealth along the narrow access road, was a compact sedan with shiny scrapes and scars across its nose, pockmarked with bullet holes along the side that he could see. It wasn't military, and unless gunmen were hiding on the floor or in the trunk, the driver was the only passenger.

"Somebody went through hell to get here," Bolan said. "We'd better find out who, and why."

Emerging from the house, he knew that it could be a trap. There was a possibility, however logically remote, that someone in authority might have sent a dented, bullet-riddled car to the house to lure the tenants out. But he could see a long stretch of the highway from the porch, and there were no more vehicles in sight. There could be infantry out there, approaching on the sly, but Pahlavi had watchers in the weeds, equipped with two-way radios and automatic weapons.

As it stood, Bolan was willing to believe the unknown driver came alone—but that wasn't the same as letting down his guard.

Not even close.

He held the AKMS ready as the car approached, watching the driver staring through his windshield at the people on the porch, while others rose from the earth, surrounding him. This was the point where he could bolt or charge the house, start shooting or attempt to ram some of Pahlavi's people with the car. But all he did was coast up to the porch, then brake and kill the engine.

Bolan waited for another moment, peering through the dusty windshield at a man he'd never seen before. Beside him, Darius Pahlavi said, "I know this man. His name is…Sherk…Sharkan…Shankara! He's another worker from the lab, on Project X!"

That said, Pahlavi leaped from the porch and ran around the car to meet its driver, as the new arrival struggled from his seat. Bolan had already observed the damage to the vehicle, and now he saw the man was wounded, dark blood soaking through his shirt and slacks, legs turning into rubber as he tried to stand.

Pahlavi caught him as he fell, joined by a couple of the others who helped lift him, carry him around the car, across the porch and inside the house. Bolan stood waiting with the others on the porch for just a moment longer, making sure no reinforcements were approaching from the highway, then he turned and went inside.

The wounded man was lying on an ancient, swaybacked sofa, talking to Pahlavi. He was exhausted, nearly out of breath and maybe out of time, but there was clearly something that he wanted to communicate. Pahlavi listened, nodding, answering in monosyllables from time to time, then raised a hand to stroke the wounded driver's head with almost loving care.

Pahlavi rose and turned to Bolan, blinking rapidly, as if he was about to cry, and said, "He tells me that Darice is still alive. Or was, some hours earlier today. He heard the chief of plant security discussing her, believing that no one could overhear him. I believe that it has killed him, but he brought the news."

"What did he hear, exactly?" Bolan asked.

"The lab security director—Kurush Gazsi is his name and he's an animal—said that Darice would be his secret weapon, even if she could not give him any information."

Bolan frowned. "You understand that doesn't mean she's still alive. He could be drawing you to rescue her, and when you get there—nothing but more guns."

"I *feel* that she still lives," Pahlavi answered, smiling now, despite the moisture on his cheeks.

"That's feeling. Knowing is something else," Bolan said.

"Of course." Pahlavi nodded. "But I have to go and find out for myself."

"Go where, exactly?" Bolan asked.

"Gazsi would keep her at the compound. There is nowhere else."

"Unless he's working with the army or police. They'll have facilities designed for a prolonged interrogation, with enhanced security."

"Gazsi would not trust anyone to do his job," Pahlavi said. "Nor would he give up the enjoyment of it."

"So, what do you want to do?" the Executioner asked.

"Proceed as planned," Pahlavi told him. "We were going to the laboratory complex anyway. Now, I have twice the reasons to succeed."

"THAT GAZSI IS A CLEVER bastard," Lieutenant Malajit Sahir said. "I give him that. Attaching locators to all the cars parked at the complex was a smart idea."

Sergeant Chandra Kalkin, hunched behind the staff car's steering wheel, did not appear convinced. "He wasn't smart enough to call us first, sir," he said.

"That was his ego undermining him," Sahir replied. "It may undo him yet. But if this turncoat leads us to the rest, it will be good for all of us."

Indeed, Sahir did not begrudge Gazsi his share of the applause, as long as Sahir got promoted, maybe decorated in the bargain, for his service to the state. The military was supposed to be a team, but for its officers, it was another dog-eat-dog environment with each man looking out for number one. Advancement was the key to a career, and in these times of Pakistan's uneasy peace with India, the only sure road to promotion was to make consistent inroads against bandits and rebels.

Saving a secret project, now, *that* should be worth a medal at the very least, and possibly a set of captain's bars.

"He's stopped," the sergeant said.

"What do you mean?"

"The car is no longer moving, sir."

"Ahead of us?"

"And to the north. Our left. He's driven off the highway, sir."

"Hurry!"

Kalkin pressed the accelerator, while Sahir palmed the dash-mounted radio's microphone, keyed the transmission button and addressed the vehicles behind him.

"We are now approaching contact," he announced. "All men, be ready. Check your weapons now and be prepared to disembark as ordered. Fire if fired upon, but otherwise, wait for my order."

The acknowledgments came back, seasoned with static. Sahir kept his eyes on the north side of the highway, watching for access roads, cart tracks, any diversion that would let their prey evade them in such open country.

"Still ahead," Kalkin said. "But we're getting closer, sir."

"I see it. On the left!" Sahir pointed, and Kalkin saw the entrance to the unpaved lane at once. Well back from the highway, at least a quarter mile from where they sat, an old house squatted in the shadow of a wooded grove.

"Stop here," Sahir commanded, reaching for his field glasses. He focused on the house, surprised at its sorry condition, even in this land of want. Nothing that he could see suggested human habitation, but the signal from their locator was clear and strong.

"I don't see any car, sir," Kalkin said.

"Nor I. He must have parked behind the house, or in the trees."

"Unless the reader is malfunctioning."

"We have to find out for ourselves. Pull in. We'll block the road with vehicles, then move up to the house on foot."

"Yes, sir."

Kalkin turned off the road and drove along the one-lane track just far enough to let the other vehicles pull in behind him. Two jeeps and an open truck followed the staff car, thirty-five armed men in all. As Sahir stepped out of his vehicle, the others tumbled from their rides and formed ranks in the nearby field.

"Our quarry," Sahir told them, pointing, "is somewhere inside that house or in the trees beyond it. We don't know why he selected this place in particular. You should assume that he is armed, and that there may be others present. Take no chances, but do everything within your power to secure at least one living prisoner. Headquarters wants to ask some questions, and they won't thank anyone who spoils their fun. Questions?"

There were none. He had not expected any.

"Very well. Fan out into a skirmish line and move on to the house. Watch out for traps along the way, man-made or otherwise. These fields are full of gullies, pits and burrows. Go!"

They went. Sahir stood watching for a moment, let his soldiers have a decent lead, then followed in their wake.

"Soldiers are coming!"

Pahlavi translated the warning from his sentry just as Bolan slipped his duffel bag into the space behind the driver's seat. He processed the alarm, retrieved his arsenal and ran back to the house, through its back door, which they had left ajar, and back into the musty sitting room where Manoj Shankara's body lay wrapped in a sheet.

Between the old house and the road, a skirmish line of troops was plodding forward, bracketing the rutted driveway, none of them apparently in any rush to reach their destination. Bolan counted thirty-two, assuming that their officer was bringing up the rear or waiting with the vehicles, perhaps with one or two close aides. Say thirty-six to make it safe, and Bolan thought the odds were reasonably good.

"Here's what we do," he told Pahlavi, speaking rapidly, his tone allowing for no argument. "Four people in the house—that's one each for the front door and two windows, with a gun on the back door. The rest, split up and fan out to the sides. Stay low, find cover and a field of fire, but don't do anything until I start the party. Got it?"

"Yes!" Pahlavi nodded briskly and began translating Bolan's orders, personally picking out the four who would remain inside. His girlfriend was one of them, and Bolan thought there was nothing wrong with that. If there was any hand-to-hand fighting outside, he wanted men up front, with their testosterone and extra body mass.

Bolan followed Pahlavi from the house, the last to leave. They both went to the left, Bolan remaining with his translator because he had no other means of speaking to the rest. He knew it was unlikely there'd be time for guidance when the shooting started, but he wanted to be ready, just in case.

They hunched and scurried through the weeds beside the old farmhouse, trusting the dusk to help them hide. When they were in position, Bolan risked a glance and saw the soldiers were fifty yards away, advancing steadily.

He didn't know how they had found the place, and at the moment Bolan didn't care. The fact was, they *had* found it, and he had to think that more troops might be en route to join the raid. It was critical to deal with these men and then get out of Dodge before the rest arrived and changed the odds beyond hope.

When the soldiers were at forty yards, Bolan palmed one of his Russian frag grenades and pulled the pin. Pahlavi, crouching ten feet to his left, glanced over at the small metallic sound it made and grimaced, turning back to face the enemy.

Still Bolan waited, knowing that his arm could only lob the lethal egg so far, and that he'd only have one chance to make a bloody first impression on his enemies. If he was early with the pitch, it would be wasted. If he stalled and dropped the grenade behind them, he might wound the stragglers without making any real dent in the skirmish line.

It had to be just right.

At twenty yards, he cocked his arm, released the safety spoon and started counting off the seconds in his head. When only three remained, he pitched the grenade overhand, then ducked back to earth with his rifle in hand to wait for the blast.

It came three seconds later, give or take. He heard a startled cry, perhaps a warning from some grunt who'd seen and recognized the danger, but it came too late. The shock of the grenade's concussion slapped his eardrums, while its shrapnel sizzled overhead. Screams radiated in a wave, and as he came erect, the AKMS leveled from his shoulder, Bolan saw a clear gap in the skirmish line.

PAHLAVI MADE his first shot count. No matter that it was almost an accident, rising beside Bolan after the grenade exploded, with his CETME rifle aimed downrange toward men who were bent on killing him this day.

He'd found a target—slender, narrow-waisted, with a vaguely dazed expression on his face after the blast—and had his sights fixed more or less upon the soldier's torso when his trigger finger slipped, the rifle bucked against his shoulder and the man went down.

This time, Pahlavi felt nothing but raw surprise, tinged with embarrassment. He had grown accustomed to the act of killing, but Pahlavi thought it shouldn't be that easy, not so casual. He ought to work for it, at least endure a moment of uncertainty verging on panic, while his adversary suffered mortal pain.

To hell with it, he thought.

He'd take what he could get, and would be glad to put this lot behind him, now that he knew his sister was still alive and subject to Kurush Gazsi's brutal attentions.

Lining up another target in the field, Pahlavi dared not let himself imagine what Gazsi had done to her. That would lead to madness, and he needed every ounce of mental clarity he possessed to make it through the next few minutes.

Pahlavi's friends were firing all at once, while soldiers on the skirmish line returned their fire, some dropping out of sight to finish the advance on hands and knees, while others fell to rise no more. The enemy's advantages were numbers, training and the possibility of calling reinforcements to the scene. That thought worried Pahlavi, and he knew it had to have been on the American's mind, as well.

The sooner they could kill these strangers and be done with it, the better his chances of escaping from the farm to save Darice.

Pahlavi fired another shot and saw his target flinch, stagger, but then keep coming. It was difficult to tell, but it appeared the hit had simply been a graze, painful but not debilitating. As the man in olive drab ducked lower, trying to conceal himself as much as possible and still keep moving forward, firing from the hip, Pahlavi tried again and this time hit him squarely in the chest.

The soldier dropped back out of sight, but someone else had glimpsed Pahlavi, and a storm of bullets rattled overhead, some passing close enough to clip the weeds around him. Death was close at hand, as it had been for days, but his fear was swallowed by determination to retrieve his sister from the hands of his enemies.

Pahlavi rolled away from where the steadily advancing

soldiers would have seen him, where they'd be expecting him to rise again. He popped up ten feet to the left and caught one of them by surprise, still firing at the spot Pahlavi had vacated. There was a split second when the young soldier appeared to realize his mistake, and then Pahlavi shot him through the neck, a puff of crimson hanging briefly in the air after he dropped from sight.

Pahlavi ducked another storm of fire, gasping this time as a slug plucked his sleeve, scorching the flesh beneath. He nearly cried out, then caught sight of Cooper kneeling in the weeds, returning hostile fire, apparently without a thought for his own safety, and Pahlavi rallied. Bending his arm to make sure it still functioned, he shook off the pain and returned to the fight.

How many soldiers still remained? Enough to win the fight, despite their losses, if his own people did not stand fast and hold the line. The house in itself meant nothing, but if they could not defeat these soldiers, then Darice was truly lost.

Pahlavi ducked as another grenade explosion rocked the firing line. Cooper had not thrown that one, and the screams that followed it were not from soldiers. Pahlavi thought he recognized them, but in the confusion of the moment he could not sort out the names, could not be sure.

Enraged, he rose above the weeds and raked the line of his advancing enemies with automatic fire. Someone was shouting curses with his voice, daring the soldiers to destroy him if they could, while gunfire rang and echoed in his ears.

THERE CAME A MOMENT in each battle when the victory was up for grabs, could still go either way, and all it took was one small shove to make the difference. When Bolan heard the second frag grenade go off and knew it wasn't one of his, he feared that point had come and might be slipping through his fingers even then, impossible to clutch and hold.

If all of the advancing soldiers started tossing frag grenades, he thought those of Pahlavi's friends who managed to survive would surely break and run. It was too much to ask of them, and if they lost heart, or if enough of them went down, it spelled the end of everything—not only Bolan's mission to prevent the ultimate success of Project X, but everything, including his life, whatever hope of final victory he harbored in his heart. The whole damned shooting match.

But after one grenade, the others never came.

He never knew what stopped them using more, whether grenades had not been properly deployed among the troops, or whether most were simply too caught up in ducking bullets and returning fire as best they could. In any case, the soldiers on the skirmish line missed their best chance to win the fight and forge ahead while dueling individually with their enemies.

It was a critical mistake.

Pahlavi's people fought from cover, four guns barking from the farmhouse, while the rest spit death through screens of grass and weeds. The vegetation couldn't shield them from incoming fire, but it obscured the soldiers' vision, spoiled their aim, while bullets flew out of the field to cut them down.

But they kept coming.

Bolan had to give them credit for determination, slogging forward as their skirmish line was pummeled, one man out of three or four already down and out. Pahlavi's team had taken hits, as well, and Bolan couldn't even start to guess their present number, but he saw that nineteen of the thirty-two soldiers he'd counted were still in the fight.

And they were getting close.

He shot another in the chest, then pivoted to catch a second as he fumbled to reload his weapon. That left seventeen that he was sure of, fit to fight—and then, they charged.

He wasn't sure if there had been an order given. There was too much shouting up and down the line in languages he didn't understand, but suddenly the rush was on, survivors rushing toward the farmhouse and the shooters who were standing in their way.

Bolan shot one more on the run, from twenty feet, then braced himself as two more closed with rifles raised like clubs. He ducked the first swing, slashed the muzzle of his AKMS into his opponent's unprotected groin, and finished with a hard knee to the face that may have snapped his neck.

The second soldier hit him on the shoulder with his rifle butt, sending a bolt of pain through Bolan's arm and chest. The warrior came close to dropping his Kalashnikov but held it with an effort, swinging in his left hand, while the tingling fingers of his right drew his Ka-bar fighting knife.

His adversary ducked, retreated, then rushed forward once again. He had his CETME rifle raised to shatter Bolan's skull, and doubtless would've done so if the Executioner had waited for the blow to fall. Instead, he lunged inside the swing and drove his blade deep into the soldier's gut, then drew it upward to his solar plexus, feeling blood and offal splash across his wrist.

The Pakistani soldier screamed and wriggled, thrashing as the blade bit deep and found his liver. Black blood followed red, and when the man fell away from Bolan, he was far past any help.

The soldier he had dropped before the last one struggled weakly on the ground, moaning, until Bolan knelt at his side and dragged the blood-slick blade across his throat. His life departed in a final shiver, leaving Bolan to confront the next soldier in line.

But there was none.

While he'd been grappling with his last two adversaries,

Bolan realized, the gunfire in the darkling field had sputtered out, gave way to sobs and grunts of fierce exertion as the last few stragglers were dispatched by hand. He scanned the field, saw no remaining enemies to slay and had a sudden flash of inspiration.

"Get their uniforms," he told Pahlavi. "Try for those that fit."

"You have a plan," Pahlavi answered with a cautious smile.

"I have a plan," Bolan replied, already staring toward the highway and its distant vehicles. "Can anybody drive those trucks?"

18

Bolan supposed his group would pass a casual inspection in the dark. Their borrowed uniforms were hardly perfect fits, but he had noticed that the soldiers he'd met so far were not exactly fashion plates. Three of the women hid long hair beneath their forage caps, while their OD fatigues concealed most other traces of their femininity. If they were smaller than the men, on average, it shouldn't matter in the vehicles, when they were sitting down.

In other circumstances, Bolan would've liked to wash the uniforms, at least remove some of the bloodstains, but again, he guessed it wouldn't matter in a truck or jeep, at night. Whichever of their enemies got close enough to notice would be killed, in any case.

The vehicles had not been damaged, which was critical, and Bolan had no shortage of capable drivers, but his team had come up short from losses in the skirmish—three dead on the firing line—so they'd been forced to leave one of the army jeeps behind. They hid it in the trees, behind the farmhouse, with Bolan's rental and Shankara's car.

Bolan had puzzled over how the troops had tracked Shankara, set Pahlavi's people to a hasty search, and thus had found the locator affixed with magnets to the undercarriage of his car. Bolan removed it and carried it with him as their para-military convoy rolled toward Project X, pausing when they were thirty miles east of the farmhouse, where he dropped it in a roadside ditch.

His enemies still might invade the farm and find his rental car, but that was low on Bolan's list of worries at the moment. He could always find another vehicle. The more important question, at the moment, was would anyone would be alive to drive it when the time came for him to depart?

They had been lucky with the opposition, so far, but he knew that they were pushing it. His team could fight, they'd definitely proved that much, and while the seventeen survivors—nineteen, with Pahlavi and himself—were groaning from the weight of surplus ammunition and grenades, the fact remained that they would be outnumbered at their target, faced not only with superior numbers and firepower, but also with various fortifications and security devices specifically designed to keep out intruders. If they couldn't breach the plant and do it with sufficient personnel to put the whole place out of action for all time, the exercise would be a bloody waste.

On top of all the obstacles that lay before them for a simple hit-and-git, Pahlavi was obsessed now with finding his sister, bringing her out alive from the viper's den. He wouldn't listen to the possibility that his informant, dying and delirious, had been mistaken—or that someone at the plant might have executed Darice after Shankara made his break.

"She is alive," he kept repeating. "I must help her. This time, *she* needs *me*."

There was no argument with that, no logic that could batter down the walls of such familial devotion. Bolan only hoped that brotherly love would not lead to Pahlavi's death—or more importantly, the failure of their mission to dismantle Project X.

Still, they were on their way and there could be no turning back. Whatever happened in the next few hours, Bolan knew that he could stand for judgment with a plea that he had done his best, unstinting in the face of killer odds. Fate might determine the result, but Bolan wasn't resting on his laurels, waiting for a signal from the Universe.

He would carry the fight to his enemies, as always, and if it should happen that he lost this time, the other side would still be candidates for massive posttraumatic stress.

Those who survived, at least.

At this instant, he was satisfied to occupy the staff car's shotgun seat and watch the dark highway unroll before their headlights. If they met another military troop in passing, Bolan was prepared to bluff. And if that failed, he was prepared to kill. More guns, grenades and ammunition for their cache, perhaps.

And they would need it all where they were going. Sight unseen, the Executioner took that on faith.

Nobody built a secret nuclear facility and left it unprotected, much less in a quasi-military state that was preparing for the war to end all wars.

Bolan couldn't aspire to that in his lifetime, but with a little skill and luck he might prevent *this* war from happening.

And that, he thought, would be enough.

DR. MEHRAN WAS WORRIED, and he didn't care who knew it. Sitting in his office with Simrin Amira and Kurush Gazsi, he felt the perspiration beading on his head, resisting the impulse to wipe it off until a salty droplet stung his eye.

"I don't see," Mehran told his chief of plant security, "how Manoj managed to escape, much less evade arrest when you had placed a beacon on his car."

"As I've attempted to explain, Doctor," Gazsi replied, "he

bluffed his way into Administration with a dummy file, claiming he was ordered to carry it by hand, then overpowered one of my men and escaped."

"That's what I can't imagine," Amira said. "Manoj couldn't overpower me, much less a trained enforcer."

"Perhaps he's managed to fool us all," Gazsi said. "Anyone can land a lucky blow or two, of course, when striking by surprise. The officers who failed to stop him will receive my personal attention, I assure you. At the same time, I believe we must consider that Manoj Shankara may be more than simply what he seems."

"Explain that," Mehran ordered.

"I'm suggesting, Doctor, that you may have had *two* spies within your plant, instead of one. Darice Pahlavi was the first to run with information from the lab. We apprehended her before she could deliver it. Now, such a short time later, comes this meek, mild-mannered nothing of a man, beating my officers unconscious, crashing through the gates and fleeing in a hail of gunfire—all for what? Simply because he had a stomachache?"

"As I've explained," Mehran said, "he requested leave for illness, and I told him to consult our staff physician for a remedy. He seemed a bit disgruntled at the time, but did not argue. I had no reason to think that he would go berserk and flee the plant. He's not that kind of man."

"As far as *you* know," Gazsi answered. "Yet, he obviously did precisely that. I would suggest to you that he was never ill, but merely used that as a ruse to get away. When you refused him… Well, we've seen what happened next."

"But why?" Mehran demanded.

"As I've said, it's my opinion that Manoj Shankara is an agent of the group called Ohm. Perhaps he was Darice

Pahlavi's handler. We may never know the full details, but I'm convinced that you have harbored traitors in the very bosom of the project all along."

Mehran saw where Gazsi was headed, but before he could respond, Amira cut through the security controller's monologue. "That won't reflect well on yourself, Kurush," she said. "Have you considered that? You've overlooked two traitors, working underneath your very nose for months on end until they start in beating up your goons. I daresay there'll be questions when you tell that story to your masters. It should be something to see."

Gazsi glared back at her while he considered his reply. "Of course," he said at last, "I'm not ascribing blame to anyone. We share the fault for failing to identify subversives whom we've seen—or, in your own case, *worked with*—every day. Apparently, they managed to deceive us all."

"There is another possibility," Amira said.

Mehran leaned forward, elbows on his desk. "What is it, Simrin?"

"For some time now," she replied, "I have suspected that Shankara was infatuated with Darice. He's had that look about him, when they were together, and I've seen him watching her at work, around the lab. I doubt she was aware of it. He's far too meek for that."

"Too meek?" Gazsi snorted. "Tell that to my man with the broken nose and the swollen—"

"Meek, I say, around the woman he's infatuated with," Amira interrupted. "Quiet with his coworkers. The kind of man who wouldn't harm an insect. But if he believed Darice had suffered harm or was in danger, well, who knows what he might do?"

"You don't believe he bought the cover story, then?" Mehran inquired.

"The tale about her marriage?" Amira shrugged. "He may have swallowed it at first, but something happened to dissuade him. Please remember that he snapped *today,* not when she disappeared, or in the intervening days. Today, I think, he heard or learned something that made him desperate."

She turned to Gazsi, saying, "Possibly, one of your men let it slip that she is still inside the compound? Or that she had been arrested. Is that possible?"

"It's possible," Gazsi said, rising. "I'll look into it at once and let you know what I find out."

"I believe you struck a nerve, Simrin," Mehran said.

She frowned. "Not that it does us any good. We still don't have a clue how to complete our work on deadline. Do we, Jamsheed?"

"No," he answered sorrowfully. "We don't."

WITH BETTER THAN a hundred miles to go, Bolan could feel the mounting urgency inside, a need to meet the enemy once more and settle all that lay between them finally, once and for all. He couldn't rush it, though. They'd reach the target when they got to it, and not a moment sooner. Speeding down the rural road at unsafe speeds would only draw attention to their convoy and risk accidents that would spoil everything.

Two hours, at their present rate of travel, meant that they would reach the lab complex before midnight. He didn't know what kind of activity they should expect, but Bolan took it for granted that security would be out in force, and they should expect a challenge on the gate.

What happened after that would depend almost equally on skill and luck, with the surprise advantage hopefully on Bolan's side. They had a heavy machine gun on the jeep, manned by one of Ohm's military veterans who had trained on the weapon a few years before, which could help swing the balance.

Beyond that, they would simply have to do their best and keep their fingers crossed.

A pair of distant headlights, moving toward them from the east, caught Bolan's eye and raised his hackles. Vehicles were not uncommon in the Pakistani hinterlands, but traveling by night was hazardous and therefore limited in most cases to military or police vehicles, bandits, or civilians caught up in emergencies. Bolan had no idea what to expect from the oncoming traffic, but he was relieved to note a single pair of headlights only, rather than another caravan.

In fact, it proved to be an old, ramshackle pickup truck with three men in the cab and half a dozen crowded in the bed behind. They might have been a labor crew returning to humble homes from a job, but from the looks they shot at Bolan's convoy, he suspected they were prowling for an easy mark, someone to rob and terrorize, mixing business and pleasure.

He would have liked to stop and question them, maybe head off a crime in progress, but they had no time for such diversions now. The crime that he had traveled halfway around the world to stop was worse than any holdup, home invasion, or whatever scheme the nine men in the old truck might have planned.

We choose our battles, Bolan thought. And maybe live to fight another day.

He'd likely never see those men again, or know what they were up to in the night. He'd never know their victims, if in fact they planned to victimize a living soul. It wasn't something he could carry on his conscience, nothing he could remedy at the expense of letting madmen set the world on fire.

"Bad men, I think," Pahlavi said.

"I think so, too," Bolan replied.

"Too bad to let them go."

"Don't let the uniform confuse you," Bolan said. "We're not the army. If the soldiers were here, they'd kill us first, and let those others go."

Pahlavi nodded. "Still."

"I hear you," Bolan said.

One job at a time. Priorities, he thought.

He focused on their target and the threat of Project X. Pahlavi didn't know how much security would be in place when they arrived, and their surprise informant from the lab had died before they'd had a chance to ask him any questions. They had floor plans for the lab and other buildings in the compound, if their diagrams were still accurate, but otherwise...

No matter.

Bolan had gone in with less at other hardsites and emerged to tell the story. Odds were only part of it. The rest lay in a winner's skill, the way he played the game.

And Bolan's enemies at Project X had never played against the Executioner.

19

Darice Pahlavi lay in darkness, weeping. They had left the light on in her cell for several hours following the latest torture session, then had doused it once again from some remote location, plunging her back into the abyss. She had lost track of time again, had no idea if it was day or night, much less how long she had been in captivity.

Her brother had to have been frantic by this time, but there was nothing he could do about it. Was there? Darius was not a fighting man, although against her better judgment he and other members of the group had purchased weapons, practiced with them under the direction of those who had served their military time. Still, it would be a joke to place Ohm in contention with the Pakistani army. They would all be slaughtered in a moment, and would have accomplished nothing with their sacrifice.

No more than I accomplished, Darice thought, with all my clever plans.

She had been foolish, thinking she could outwit Gazsi and the rest, but she had acted on her conscience and was not ashamed of that. Her only shame was failing when her friends and family, her countrymen—perhaps the very world itself—depended on her to succeed.

Too late.

Her future had been hedged and narrowed to a darkened tunnel, lighted only by intense flashes of agony from time to time, which led inevitably to the grave. It was too late for her to spread the word of Project X, but maybe Darius and Ohm could do it, even if they lacked the final proof.

Perhaps *someone* would listen to the truth, before it was too late.

She heard the footsteps coming back and gasped in fear. It was too soon! They couldn't have more questions yet, after so short a time.

It had to be Gazsi, she decided. He enjoyed tormenting her in every way he could, because Darice had spurned his amorous advances more than once. He had her at his mercy now, and nothing that he did to her would lead to any form of discipline for him, because he acted in the name of state security.

She braced herself, preparing for the pain and the humiliation. If the light had still been on, she might have grabbed the slop bucket and flung it at him, but she could not find it quickly in the pitch-darkness of her cell. Instead, she sat up trembling on her cot and faced the general direction of the doorway, face set in a grim expression that she hoped would indicate defiance. Naked as she was, the gesture might be wasted, but it was the best that she could do.

A key scraped in the lock, and as the door swung open, so the light above her blazed on, chasing midnight shadows to the corners of the room. Gazsi stood over her, flanked by his men, examining her body with a look of casual disinterest—and something else.

Was that concern? Even a touch of fear?

"Manoj Shankara," he declared.

It took a moment for Darice to wrap her mind around the

words, identify them as a name, then remember that she knew the man whose name it was.

"Is that a question?" she replied.

"It is a name."

"I know that."

"You know *him*."

"From working only. Yes."

She hoped that merely knowing her and working with her would not land Shankara in a prison cell, but there was nothing she could do to help him from her cage.

"He fled the plant today," Gazsi informed her. "Knocked one of my guards unconscious, crashed his car through both the gates, outran pursuit. There was a beacon in his car, but he discovered it. We've found it miles away, tossed in a roadside ditch."

"You've had a bad week altogether," Darice said, smiling for the first time since she had been arrested.

"It amuses you?"

"Why not? Are you a friend of mine?"

"I could be," Gazsi said, "despite the recent unpleasantness between us. I can help you, maybe even reinstate you, but before that happens you must first help me."

"Your generosity is overwhelming," Darice said. "What must I do?"

"Explain Shankara's role in Ohm, how long he has been spying on the project, who his contacts are. Above all else, tell me where he has gone."

Darice was startled by the laughter welling out of her. It made her breasts shake, sparked new stabs of pain between her battered ribs and lower down, but she could not contain it. It was simply too hilarious.

"Manoj a spy!" she said at last, when she could draw a

breath to speak. "You've lost your mind. They'll come replace you soon, when they discover you're insane."

Gazsi leaped forward, punched her in the face, slamming her back across the cot. Dazed though she was, Darice could hear him shouting at her as if from a thousand yards away.

"Insane, am I? We'll see about that! Bring the generator and the cables! Now! Goddamn you, move when I say move!"

EXHAUSTED, THROAT SORE from shouting, Gazsi slumped into his office chair, drumming his fingers on the tidy desktop. Waves of anger and frustration made him dizzy, as if he was on a ship at sea, the concrete floor a rolling deck beneath his chair.

His latest session with the traitor had been a total waste of time. The urgency of his superiors' demands had stolen all the guilty pleasure from it, and on top of that she had known nothing worth the effort. So, she worked beside Shankara on a daily basis and had voiced her reservations about Project X in confidence. Shankara was infatuated with the bitch, and thus had not reported her disloyal remarks, but if he was in fact a member of the group called Ohm, Darice Pahlavi was not aware of it. In fact, she took it as a joke—at least, until the alligator clips had been strategically applied.

But if Shankara *wasn't* part of Ohm, why had he fled the plant? Why risk a bullet to the brain or worse, if he was not involved in the conspiracy?

Simrin Amira's words came back to him. "Today, I think, he heard or learned something that made him desperate."

But *what?*

What, in a normal working day, would turn a meek lab rat into a tiger?

Shankara was in love with the girl, Gazsi thought, albeit a

one-sided, unrequited sort of puppy love. Her disappearance would have agitated him, but he had appeared to buy the cover story Gazsi had concocted after Darice was arrested.

What had changed his mind?

He heard or learned something that made him desperate.

Heard what? From whom? What could produce such desperation in a man so meek, unless—

The pieces fell together with such sudden clarity that Gazsi feared he might be ill. He thought about Shankara's bid to leave the plant that day, pleading an ailment of his bowels. Then Gazsi saw himself, together with an aide, washing their hands together in the men's room while he blathered on about Darice, his plan to use her for bait to trap her brother and the rest.

Gazsi believed that he had checked the toilet stalls for occupants before he spoke—it was a habit he had cultivated over time—but *had* he, really? There was no way to be sure, and if Shankara had been listening…

Then he would know Darice was still alive, in danger, likely suffering. And he would know that Gazsi planned to treat her brother much the same.

Something that made him desperate.

And it was Gazsi's fault.

If he was right, his negligence lay at the root of all their troubles. First, he'd failed to catch Darice consorting with her friends at Ohm, then he had launched a bumbling would-be savior out into the countryside. Shankara could not help Darice, of course, but what if he had some means of contacting Darius Pahlavi and the others? Even if he wasn't part of Ohm, they might be casual acquaintances. Perhaps Darice had told him where to go and who to see, in the event of an emergency.

If that was the case, it struck a third and fatal blow at Gazsi, since his multiple interrogations had produced no evidence of such a fallback plan, no desperate admission that Darice had roped Shankara into her pathetic web of plotters. Even when Gazsi had asked her the specific questions, she'd denied it.

Could a woman be that strong?

In other circumstances, Gazsi would have relished finding out, but there was no more time to waste on children's games. He decided no one could ever know how his carelessness had undermined the project, in its most crucial stage. The penalty for failure on that scale would go beyond dismissal, to the dungeon and the execution chamber.

His best hope, all things considered, was to keep the plant secure while Mehran and the others worked their magic in the lab. They had a deadline looming, and if Mehran failed to meet it while the plant stood safe and sound, it would be *his* neck on the chopping block, not Gazsi's.

As it should be.

Smiling to himself without conviction, Kurush Gazsi rose and hurried back to work.

"WE'RE ALMOST THERE," Pahlavi said. "Perhaps half a mile more."

That meant their headlights would be visible to the compound guards before much longer. "Stop here," said Bolan. "Kill the lights."

"Right here?"

"Right here, right now."

Pahlavi stopped the staff car, switching off its engine and headlights. A signal to the jeep and truck behind them brought the miniconvoy to a halt in darkness, engines ticking as they cooled. The motley troops unloaded, clustered around Bolan and Pahlavi on the shoulder of the two-lane highway.

"Translate for me, will you?" Bolan asked Pahlavi.

"Yes."

"We haven't got much time," he told the others. "Half a mile ahead of us, maybe a little less, they're waiting at the complex. We don't know how many guards they have, whether they're army regulars or private mercenaries, and we only have a general idea of how they're armed."

He waited for Pahlavi to catch up. The faces that surrounded them were pale and grim by moonlight, but he didn't see a quitter in the bunch.

"I won't pretend that what we're trying will be easy," Bolan said. "It won't. Some of you likely won't be going home again. You've lost friends already, just this afternoon, and there's no way to cut the losses if you go ahead. This is a killing place. The only question left is who gets killed and who survives."

Another pause with Pahlavi translating. Bolan saw shifting in the ranks, but no one turned away.

"You all know why we're here," Bolan added a moment later. "First, it's Project X. To stop the bomb. And now, on top of that, we have a search-and-rescue mission." Glancing toward Pahlavi, he continued. "I want all of you to recognize priorities. If we retrieve the lady, but we miss the bomb, it means we may as well have stayed at home. Because she'll be dead anyway, along with all of you and everyone you love."

Some of the Ohm members were exchanging glances, but they all stood firm. Pahlavi's voice was steady, making Bolan wonder if he'd translated verbatim, but he had no way to double-check it. If his guide was substituting other words for Bolan's, they were well and truly screwed.

"You've proved that you can fight. I'm satisfied with that,"

Bolan said. "And I know you're not afraid to die. Remember, though, that martyrs never won a war. They just get in the way. You trip over their bodies and get killed, yourself. We don't need corpses. We need soldiers."

Several of the young commandos nodded at that, while others muttered what Bolan took for assent. Once again, none retreated.

"When we pull up to the gates," he told them, "I expect floodlights to hit us right away. We'll have a moment, give or take, before they realize that something's wrong. We need to use that time and take them by surprise. I'll take the first shot, and we'll rush the gate in the staff car. Take out the lights and any tower guards as best you can with the machine gun. After that, when we're inside, you know the drill."

They had been over it enough, using the floor plans. If they didn't know it now, they never would.

"Don't worry if it feels like Hell in there tonight. It always feels like that in combat. It's supposed to feel that way. You need to be the biggest, baddest devils in the mix. Roll over anybody in your way and keep them down. All right?"

This time, his fighters answered with a single voice, albeit on a time delay, after Pahlavi gave them the translation. There were words he couldn't understand mixed in there, but the tone and the expressions on their faces told him they were ready.

At least, as ready as they'd ever be.

He didn't think about which ones of them would die within the next half hour, or whether any of them would survive. That kind of thinking was defeatist, and it had no place in combat other than a mission recognized from the get-go as suicide.

That wasn't Bolan's game. Not in the past, and not this night. He wanted to survive, to bring as many of these people out alive as possible. He'd even like to meet Pahlavi's sister and escort her from the hell where she'd been caged for days on end.

But at the bottom line, he'd come to scuttle Project X, and nothing took priority over that goal. Not damsels in distress, not youngsters playing soldier for the first time in their lives.

Not even life itself.

20

As Bolan had expected, the lab compound was ablaze with lights as they approached. From one mile out, it sparked his memory of clips from science-fiction films—a lonely outpost in the desert, lit with candlepower that would make it visible from outer space, technicians waiting for first contact with a master race from who knew where. Unlike the movie scientists, however, those in charge of Project X were moving toward a close encounter of the Bolan kind.

And none of them would ever be the same again.

There was no point trying to conceal the convoy as it rolled toward the site. Quite the reverse, in fact. The benefit of stealing army vehicles was the advantage of surprise. They left the headlights on and made a straight run toward the gates, where soldiers armed with automatic weapons waited to receive them.

Bolan wasn't sure how such things worked in Pakistan, but in the United States, an officer would typically announce his visit to a top-secret facility—unless there was some reason why he needed to surprise the folks in charge. Arriving in the middle of the night, completely unexpected, Bolan's convoy thus would tweak the paranoia of the plant's defenders, make them wonder if they had a problem.

And by the time they recognized the trick, with any luck, it would already be too late.

A sentry left the gate to intercept them while the beams of two searchlights converged on Bolan's vehicles. He reckoned that the tower guards would need binoculars to spot the bloodstains on the uniforms Pahlavi's people wore, and even if they had field glasses, he was not about to give them time for searching scrutiny.

The guard approached, gun drawn, to ask Pahlavi what was going on, and Bolan shot him in the face. They had discussed the plan, but still Pahlavi flinched for just an instant, then recovered, gripped the staff car and stamped on the accelerator pedal.

They shot forward, engine snarling, even as the big machine gun on the jeep behind them started chattering. One of the searchlights instantly went dark, and Bolan glimpsed one of its operators tumbling from his high perch like a rag doll, cartwheeling through space. He didn't track the body all the way to impact, though, for they were smashing through the gate by then, chain link scraping along the staff car's flanks and leaving claw marks on the paint.

The second gate was just a wooden arm that raised and lowered on command. Pahlavi snapped it off and sent it flying, while the soldiers stationed at the checkpoint dived for cover, two or three of them unleashing wild shots as they fled.

Bolan caught one of them retreating, ripped him with a burst from his Kalashnikov and sent the dead man sprawling. In his mirror, he could see the jeep and truck already through the gate and following, lit up with muzzle-flashes, raising hell with the defenders who came rushing out to stop them.

By agreement, they were racing toward the building labeled "B" on Pahlavi's map of the compound. It was supposed to be the main lab where the techs of Project X worked overtime to make their corner of the world a bleak, irradiated wasteland.

Bolan didn't bother analyzing people so committed to the spread of pain and death. He didn't judge their motives or attempt to read their minds. If they were someone's father, brother, uncle, cousin, it was all the same to him. Their crimes against humanity outweighed the rest of it.

He simply killed them and moved on.

But first, he'd have to get inside the lab, and that would be no easy task. Already, guards were spilling out of doorways everywhere he looked, racing to intercept the convoy of intruders, firing as they ran. The car was taking hits, and Bolan knew the truck behind him made an even better target.

Just another moment.

Pahlavi braked as they approached the lab, and Bolan vaulted from the car, not waiting for the rest. He lobbed a frag grenade toward the defenders ranged in front of him, and hit the deck as sudden thunder tore the night apart.

GAZSI WAS FLUSHED with panic as he stumbled out of the administration building, suddenly confronted with a scene straight out of Hell. The gates were down—or, rather, torn apart and cast aside—with bodies sprawling on the ground around them. Two searchlights were dark, the earth below their towers strewed with shattered glass and one more twisted corpse. Away to Gazsi's left, three military vehicles were racing toward the main lab, spewing gunfire, while the camp's defenders sprayed the vehicles with bullets.

Stunned by what he saw, giddy from breathing cordite fumes, Gazsi could not imagine what was happening—unless, perhaps, there was a coup in progress, rebels from the army trying to depose the sitting government. He thought of Ohm and instantly dismissed it. How would peasant rebels get their hands on army weapons, uniforms and vehicles?

But if this *was* a coup, however ill-conceived, it might foretell a change in leadership. If it succeeded, Gazsi and the other personnel of Project X might not be treated with the same consideration they had heretofore been shown.

In short, he reckoned it was time to leave.

But not alone.

A measure of insurance wouldn't hurt in case he had to bargain with the rebels or civilian enemies of the regime. His possibilities were limited, but one came instantly to mind.

Gazsi had brought his pistol with him, when he heard the sounds of gunfire. Nothing else inside the administration building mattered to him. He had to reach Darice Pahlavi without getting killed along the way, release her from her cell, and march her to his car. The rebels had already cleared his access route to the outside, and they would doubtless keep the other guards engaged while Gazsi slipped away, unnoticed in the chaos.

He had no idea where they would go, as yet, but he would think of something on the road. Gazsi had bank accounts, if he could access them in time, and two spare passports in a safe-deposit box, but he could always try his luck at crossing over into India by covert means. If necessary, he could sell his services to the New Delhi bureaucrats, a convert who could tell them all about the Pakistani threat and help them prove it if they took their case to the United Nations.

Anything, in short, to keep himself alive.

But first, he had to reach Darice Pahlavi and extract her from her cell, compel her to cooperate if she valued her own life.

And if she didn't, well, Gazsi would take her with him, anyway. She simply had no choice.

Gunfire echoed throughout the compound, and the remaining searchlights swept across the scene erratically, seeking elusive targets. Gazsi dodged the lights and clung to shadows, trying to be inconspicuous as he traversed the compound. He was known to all the soldiers assigned to Project X, but he could not tell who they were in the confusion of the moment, and he did not care to meet a group of rebels if he could help it. They might cut him down on sight, or else detain him for interrogation if they had the time and manpower to spare. In either case, the outcome did not fit with Gazsi's plans.

Running in fits and starts, he made his way across the compound like a sneak thief, dodging men in uniform wherever they appeared, clutching his pistol in a trembling hand. A headache throbbed behind his eyes, exacerbated by the sounds of gunfire, but he had no remedy.

Escape was all that mattered.

The sole alternative was death.

DARIUS PAHLAVI FIRED a short burst from his CETME assault rifle, cursing as his bullets missed their moving target and struck sparks from the pavement. He tried again, catching the soldier as he swung around, attempting to return fire, this time stitching him across the chest to drop him where he stood.

It was chaotic in the compound, figures dashing here and there in military uniforms, only their faces serving to distinguish friend from foe when there was time or light enough to see them. Pahlavi and his ally had considered making simple armbands for their comrades, then discarded the idea as it might simply help the compound's defenders spot their targets on the run. So far, Pahlavi hadn't shot one of his friends, and trusted that the odds against them—heavily outnumbered as they were—would help prevent his doing so.

He couldn't get Darice out of his mind, but had no clue where Gazsi might be holding her inside the complex. She would not be in the lab, that much was fairly certain, but the layout also featured barracks, offices, a mess hall and substantial storage space. Pahlavi might be forced to search it all before he found his sister, yet he couldn't start that vital exercise until he had helped raze the lab.

Despite the pain it caused him, Pahlavi knew that scuttling Project X was more important to the outside world than any single person's life.

The anger spawned by that idea gave him new energy and focus as he fought his way around one corner of the laboratory building, toward the entrance.

Bolan was ahead of him, lobbing another antipersonnel grenade and crouching low as it exploded, shrapnel whining through the smoky air. Pahlavi saw the guards and soldiers scattered by its blast, writhing in blood and other fluids he was unable to name.

Bolan advanced, Pahlavi on his heels, three others close behind them, firing bursts in all directions as new targets came into their view. Incoming fire chipped at the wall behind them, spraying them with concrete shards, but thus far none of them had suffered any major wounds.

Pahlavi didn't know about the rest of his comrades. They'd scattered, leaping from their vehicles, except for Darshan on the jeep's heavy machine gun. From the sound of it, the soldiers had not dropped him yet, but he could only last so long, a stationary target ringed by enemies. Pahlavi hoped Darshan would save himself, but there was nothing he could do to help his old friend now.

Frustration gnawed inside his stomach as they crept by inches toward the main lab's entrance, ducking gunfire all the way.

When they were close enough, Bolan lobbed yet another hand grenade, this one exploding on the very threshold of the lab and buckling its doors so that they hung ajar and twisted in their frame. Bright muzzle-flashes from inside marked the position of the defenders, and Pahlavi answered with his rifle, emptying one magazine and reaching for another at his waist.

Janna edged closer to him, worry written on her face, clinging white-knuckled to her submachine gun as she huddled in Pahlavi's shadow. "What about Darice?" she called to him above the racket of the guns.

"Later," he answered bitterly, "if there is time. The bomb comes first."

"You have such courage," she replied, forcing a smile.

Pahlavi saw the love reflected in her eyes and hoped she saw the same in his. He hoped, also, that they would have more time together, once this Hell on Earth was behind them. But he knew they couldn't count on it.

"Stay close," he said. "We're almost there."

And turning from the woman who had sworn to be his wife someday, Pahlavi followed the big American toward the laboratory doors.

A SWIRL OF SMOKE met Bolan as he crossed the threshold to the structure labeled "B" on their hand-drawn strategic maps of the compound. It didn't smell like any chemicals were burning yet—except the ones in gunpowder and high explosives—but he kept his breathing shallow all the same, as he pushed past the crooked hanging doors and made his way inside.

Gunfire erupted instantly and drove him to the floor. There was no need to warn the others, crowding in behind him, as the bullets whistled overhead, smacking the walls and doors. He heard Pahlavi shouting at the woman called Janna, then felt bodies jostling all around him, each looking for his or her piece of the deck.

Bolan saw muzzle-flashes up ahead, winking around a counter and a turnstile where, he guessed, employees had been checked through to their jobs each morning and checked out again as they were leaving for the day. He wasn't sure how many shooters held the checkpoint, but their cover was superior and Bolan didn't feel like charging down the muzzles of their guns if he could help it.

He reached down to his belt and found another Russian hand grenade—his second last, before he'd have to use the larger models he'd retrieved from Pakistani troops who didn't need them anymore. It was a second's work to free the safety pin and drop it, glance at his allies to either side and let them see what he was doing, then rear back and make the pitch.

It wasn't perfect—few things ever were in combat—but it did the job. From where he lay, Bolan saw the grenade bounce once, across a countertop beside the turnstile, then drop out of sight among his enemies. Some of them recognized it, shouting in a sudden panic as they tried to flee, but no athlete on Earth could travel far enough to save himself within the time remaining.

Bolan rode the shock wave of the blast and kept his head down while the shrapnel sang around him. Most of it stayed well behind the checkpoint barrier, but some punched through, while other fragments peppered walls and punctured the acoustic ceiling tiles. Beyond the checkpoint, automatic fire gave way to screams and gurgling cries of pain.

Bolan was on his feet a heartbeat later, rushing toward the turnstile, leaping over it to crouch among the dead and dying. There were five, bleeding freely from a dozen wounds. Pahlavi knelt beside one and clutched his hair in one hand, brandishing his rifle in the other, hammering away with questions. When the wounded man replied with a weak head shake, clearly pleading ignorance, Pahlavi left him to die.

"I had to ask about Darice," he said. "You understand?"

Bolan nodded, reminding him, "We've still got work to do."

"I'm here," Pahlavi said. "Let's do it now."

They moved forward together, pressed against opposing walls, advancing step by step. Bolan reviewed the floor plans in his mind, surprised to find that they were accurate in scrupulous detail. Pahlavi's sister had invested time and effort in those plans, and it had cost her dearly.

Bolan hoped they'd have a chance to help her, but he knew he couldn't guarantee it. They still had at least one bomb to find and decommission before they could pursue Pahlavi's private quest. Until that job was done, it claimed their top priority.

In front of Bolan, six or seven feet away, a door flew open and expelled three lab technicians in white coats. One woman and two men, all looking panicked and confused to find themselves stuck in the middle of a firefight. Bolan saw his opportunity and leapt to grab one of the technicians by his collar, dragging him back toward the open room he had just evacuated.

"Get the others," he told Pahlavi. "They can lead us to the bomb!"

21

Dr. Mehran was terrified. His body trembled from his quaking legs, up to his chattering teeth, a panic reaction he couldn't suppress, despite the embarrassment it caused him. Simrin Amira, standing close beside him in the closet, did not seem to notice, but Mehran knew she had to feel him shaking, judging him a coward as they stood together in the dark.

The closet had been her choice for a hiding place, of course, and Mehran had agreed because the sound of gunfire and explosions made his mind go blank. He seemed incapable of forming a coherent thought, even to save himself. But now that they were actually in the closet, with what sounded like a full-scale war raging outside, Mehran believed that trusting Amira may have been his last mistake.

The first—or the most critical, at least—had been when he agreed to work on Project X. Seduced by money, flattery and patriotic zeal, Mehran had signed on to the program without really thinking of the risks to himself, to his country, or to the world at large. Now, when it seemed that Project X was going to collapse around his ears and bury him, he wished that he had been a wiser, stronger man.

Too late.

He'd thrown that chance away, and now he found himself

standing in a pitch-dark closet with a woman who most likely thought he was a fool, waiting for strangers to burst in and kill him where he stood. Great plans came down to nothing in the end, all vanity and empty posturing, he thought.

"I'm not sure this was such a good idea," Amira said.

"You thought of it!"

"I know that! But I think, now, we should try to make our way outside."

"Through that?" He pointed toward the doorway and the battle sounds beyond it, even knowing that Amira could not see the gesture. "How?"

"They're fighting with the guards," she answered. "If we stay low, run like hell, why should they bother us?"

"They're attacking *the lab*," he reminded her. "Don't you suppose we'll be targets?"

"Better moving targets, then, than sitting ducks."

"I don't know…if I can," Mehran replied.

"Can what?" Amira asked.

Tears streaming down his face, he said, "I'm not sure I can move, much less…I mean…"

Somehow, her hand found his and squeezed. Remarkably, Mehran discovered that her touch calmed him. The hand she held stopped trembling almost instantly, together with the arm attached to it. If she would only wrap her arms and legs around him now, perhaps—

That fantasy went nowhere, as a bullet drilled the closet door and smacked into the wall a foot from Amira's head. He ducked instinctively, knees cracking, tightening his grip on Simrin's hand until she whimpered from the sudden pain.

"Sorry!" he whispered.

"Never mind. We're getting out of here, right now."

"But, where—?"

"Shut up and follow me!"

The door opened a second later, Amira's free hand was on the knob, and Mehran felt her dragging him along behind her, out and to their left along the so-familiar corridor. He wasn't sure where she might lead him, but it hardly seemed to matter at the moment, with the sounds of gunfire ringing in his ears.

A pair of Gazsi's guards rushed past them, headed in the opposite direction, paying no attention to Mehran or Amira. Both had rifles braced against their shoulders, eyes narrowed behind plastic goggles, mouths set in grim snarls. Mehran was glad to see the last of them, and that they had ignored him, but as Amira led him farther down the hallway, he could only wonder what still lay ahead.

DARICE PAHLAVI HEARD the distant, muffled sounds of gunfire, but the racket barely penetrated through the haze that fogged her mind. Someone was shooting, she could work out that much, but as far as who it might've been and why they should be shooting at that time of—day? night? whatever it was—she had no clue.

A part of her, still rational, assumed that it had to be important, otherwise no one would fire a gun around the laboratory complex. But her situation was so hopeless, her defenses beaten down by cruel abuse, that she could not put two and two together for a logical result.

She recognized the sound of footsteps in the hallway, though, and understood their import perfectly. The tick-tock of their swift approach made Darice slump back on her cot and draw her legs into a fetal curl. Weeping, she waited for the door to open, wondering if it would be the final time. A moment later, Gazsi stood above her in a glare of light, but even with her eyelids closed to slits, Darice saw that this time he was alone.

"We're leaving," he informed her. "Can you walk, or must I call a man to drag you?"

"Walk?" The concept struck her as eccentric. Gazsi may as well have asked if she could swing from a trapeze.

"That's right. Assuming you still want to live." He drew a pistol, cocked it, aiming in the general direction of her tear-streaked face. "Or I can leave you here, after ensuring that you'll never speak about our time together. It's your choice, Darice."

With something close to superhuman will, she struggled to her feet. The world began to tilt, but with her arms outstretched she managed not to fall. It was a tightwire act. Perhaps she *could* manage the trapeze, after all.

Gazsi held out a lab coat. "Put this on," he ordered.

Suddenly remembering that she was nude, Darice snatched at the coat, half turned away from him and struggled into it. The buttons were a puzzle, taking more time than they had to spare, and Gazsi snapped at her to finish them along the way.

"We're going now," he said. "Do what I tell you, when I tell you, and you may yet see the brother you admire so much."

"Darius? Is he here?" The very notion staggered her.

"Not here," Gazsi said. "We must go to meet him."

"Yes, please," she replied.

Gripping her right hand with his left, so that she had no chance to finish buttoning her lab coat, Gazsi led Darice out of the cell that she'd begun to think of as her final home. The corridor seemed chilly, with its air-conditioning. She shivered, then fell into step behind Gazsi as he began to move along the hallway.

Darice didn't ask where they were going. Anything was better than her cell and the interrogation room, where she'd been strapped down on a table while they—

No!

She wouldn't think about that now. She needed all her

courage for whatever was about to happen next. The gun in Gazsi's hand and the continued sounds of shooting, louder now, told her some kind of battle had been joined within the lab. It made no sense, and yet—

Perhaps it *did* make sense, she thought. If Ohm had gathered strength enough to stage a raid, try something, anything, to shut down Project X, it might not be too late.

Too late for what? her mind echoed.

And yet another small voice answered back, For me. For all of us.

BOLAN ASKED THE QUESTIONS, while Pahlavi translated, his tone and attitude swiftly persuading the technicians that they should cooperate. They answered his inquiries, and Bolan listened to Pahlavi's clipped rendition.

"They have been placed on a deadline. None of them believe it can be done. Two weeks. Ridiculous they say."

Pahlavi snapped at them again, jabbing the muzzle of his CETME rifle into one man's gut, and listened to the torrent they unloaded in response.

"They claim the weapon has not been completed. They have the materials. No, some of the materials. It's difficult to understand, when they... Something retards their progress. I'm not sure—"

"It's okay," Bolan told him. "I don't care what's slowed them. Do you believe them?"

Stepping back a pace from his three prisoners, Pahlavi studied them for several seconds, gunfire hammering throughout the other nearby rooms, then nodded. "Yes," he said at last. "They're very frightened. I believe them."

"Then we only need to see the parts they've finished, deal with those and trash the lab," Bolan replied. "Simple."

"Simple," his guide repeated, heavy on the irony. Another whiplash order from him made the three technicians cringe from him, then slowly nod agreement.

"They will show us where the pieces are," Pahlavi said. "They want to live."

"Okay. Let's go."

"And after that—?"

"Darice," Bolan assured him, thinking, *If there's time. If we still can.*

The technicians led Bolan and Pahlavi from the makeshift grilling room, clearly reluctant to approach the battleground, but prodded from behind with weapons and Pahlavi's threats of instant death if they refused. Bolan surveyed the scene as they proceeded down another corridor, observing that his goal of taking out the labs had nearly been accomplished in his absence, by the seesaw struggle for control. Bullets and shrapnel had destroyed much of the delicate equipment, punctured walls and ceiling panels, shattered furniture. It wasn't permanent—they'd need plastique or fire for that—but no one would be building any weapons in that wreckage for the next few weeks, at least.

Bolan considered, once again, the prospect that a bullet or grenade might crack a cabinet or canister containing nuclear material, exposing them all to radiation in a killing dose, but there was nothing he could do about it. He'd discussed the problem with Pahlavi's people at the house, and they'd all agreed to take the risk, while making every effort to avoid contamination of their comrades and themselves.

Some of it still came down to luck, and Bolan wasn't sure how much his side had left.

Their three reluctant guides brought Bolan and Pahlavi to a short, plain corridor some distance from the rooms where men and women were engaged in killing one another, giving it their best. One of the male technicians tapped in numbers on a keypad by the last door on their left, then pushed his way inside. The others followed, trailed by Bolan and Pahlavi, Bolan pausing long enough to knock a trash can over with his foot and use it as a wedge, to keep the door from swinging shut behind them.

Even with his lack of expertise in items nuclear, the Executioner recognized the place. There was the glove box, where technicians stood with arms inserted through stout, insulated sleeves to handle dangerous materials. Another one had robot arms, controlled from the outside by joysticks. The wall to Bolan's left was lined with HAZMAT suits, dangling from stainless-steel hooks. The floor beneath their feet was spotless.

Within that room lay the components for a weapon that, while relatively small, could someday rock the world—and maybe even dam the stream of human history. The Doomsday elves hadn't assembled it, so far, but Bolan recognized some of the parts. Together, finished, they were Hiroshima in a handbag. Nagasaki at rush hour.

The troops Pahlavi's team had vanquished at the house had come well prepared, although they'd left some of their best gear in their vehicles. The Willie Pete, for example. Their white phosphorous grenades. Thermite.

Bolan palmed one and passed another to Pahlavi, nodding for the technicians to leave. "Let's shake and bake," he said. "We haven't got all night."

22

Pahlavi turned his face away from the fierce heat of the burning laboratory, eyes half closed against the glare of chemical explosions. The incendiary grenades were incredible, white-hot chunks of phosphorous melting steel and burning through concrete as if it was cardboard. The fireworks show had brought a momentary lull in fighting, as defenders and invaders alike gaped in wonder, momentarily awed by the awesome display of destruction.

Bolan had explained that the thermite charges should destroy all weapons-grade material within the plant, along with the peripheral components, tools and plans required to build a bomb. It would not—*could not*—wipe the knowledge from the minds of those technicians who had worked on Project X, but some of them were probably incinerated by the blast, and Pahlavi planned to shoot any he saw from that point onward.

While he searched the compound for his sister.

Pahlavi knew he might not find her, at the very least might not find her alive, but he was bound to try.

"Ready when you are," Bolan said, as if he could read Pahlavi's mind.

Pahlavi looked around the compound, saw the guards and soldiers still engaged in fighting members of his team at several points. The numbers had thinned on both sides, since they'd crashed the gates twelve minutes earlier. Janna was still alive and at his side, but he could count three dead among his friends from where he stood.

"I don't know where to start," he answered bitterly.

"Think of the layout," Bolan said. "She wasn't in the main lab, which leaves four buildings to search."

Four, Pahlavi thought. It might as well have been four hundred. "I don't know!"

"Administration's where we entered. Do you think they'd hold her near their offices?" Bolan asked.

It seemed unlikely. "No," Pahlavi said, shaking his head.

"Okay, what's left. In Building C, you've got the kitchen, dining room and library."

"Not there," Pahlavi guessed. "Too much foot traffic every day. Too many witnesses."

"D is the barracks," Bolan said.

A possibility, Pahlavi thought, but what about the guards and other staff in residence, who came and went from tiny sleeping rooms a dozen times each day? Gazsi would not want them distracted by the fuss and noise of an interrogation, would he?

"No," he finally replied.

"That narrows down the search to E," Bolan said. "Storage and maintenance."

Perfect. Aside from storage rooms, Pahlavi realized, they would have privacy and tools. Tears stung his eyes as he said, "I will search E next."

"Makes sense to me," the Executioner agreed.

But first, they had to get there, and the battle for the compound had not ended with the fiery destruction of the lab. If anything, the compound's defenders seemed to have redoubled their efforts, as if seeking revenge now that they'd missed their chance to avert disaster.

Their heavy machine gun had fallen silent, and while Pahlavi didn't know what that meant for Darshan, he couldn't go and check on his good friend before he sought Darice.

Facing Bolan and the rest who gathered round him, huddled in the depth of shadows next to Building C, Pahlavi said, "I need to find my sister. This is my fight only. You may leave if you wish to. All of you have reason to be proud, and seeking safety now should not embarrass you."

Janna pressed forward, stormy-eyed, seeming as if she was about to slap him. "You insult us, Darius!" she snapped. "You think that we would leave you now? That I would leave you?"

"But—"

"We go together. Now."

Bolan didn't understand the words but the young woman's intentions were clear.

Pahlavi nodded, blinking back another swell of tears, though not from anguish this time. Studying the battlefield in front of him, he waited for an opening. Not looking for a lull in gunfire, but the opposite—a flare-up in some other portion of the compound that would keep his enemies distracted while his small team raced toward Building E.

A moment later, a grenade explosion from the general direction of the gates drew guards and soldiers in that direction, several firing as they ran, although Pahlavi could not guess their targets. If they had a party of his friends cornered, he wished the others well and vowed to help them soon. Or else avenge them, if it came to that.

He glanced at Bolan, caught a nod from the American.

"It's time," Pahlavi told the others, lunging from the shadows even as he spoke the order. "Follow me!"

Seconds into the advance, the team met opposition from a clutch of soldiers hanging out near Building D. Firing in twos and threes, the enemy peppered the parking lot and drove the Ohm commandos off their course, looking for cover on the near side of the same building.

That made it tricky. They could theoretically be stuck all night in that position—or until the camp's defenders rallied to surround and wipe them out—and Bolan reckoned they were quickly running out of time. Some kind of breakthrough was required, and he decided it was his job to provide it.

"Hold them here," he told Pahlavi. "I'll cut through the barracks and surprise them. Shake them up a little. When they're hopping, you can close the trap."

Pahlavi blinked at him. "It should be I who—"

"You've got business waiting for you," Bolan cut him off. "This is my specialty."

"Just one of them, I think," Pahlavi said.

"Wait here, unless they try to box you. You'll know when I get there."

"Right. Good luck!" Pahlavi said.

There was an entrance to the barracks ten feet to the left. Bolan went through it in a crouch and moved along an east-west corridor that led him toward the corner where his enemies had taken up position. Doors lined either side, most of them closed as Bolan passed, no sounds inside the barracks rooms to indicate that anyone was home. Of course, that didn't mean—

A door flew open on his left, and Bolan glimpsed a pistol thrusting toward his face. He dropped and rolled, the first explosion well above him and its bullet wasted, drilling through another door directly opposite.

He fired a short burst from the floor, saw drywall pulverized, and then his enemy in olive drab was angling for another shot, dropping the pistol's muzzle toward the floor where Bolan lay. He rolled again, barely before the muzzle-flash, and fired once more on his rotation, as his shoulder hit the wall.

His second burst went in on target, more or less. It cut the shooter's legs from under him and dropped him to the floor, alive but stunned and gasping on the brink of shock. The pistol wavered, wobbled as its owner tried for target acquisition one more time, but Bolan didn't let him get there.

Firing from a range of six or seven feet, he put two bullets through the wounded soldier's face and finished it. Blood splashed the wall behind his target's head before the dead man slumped sideways and let his pistol drop from twitching fingers.

That had been too close for comfort, Bolan thought, and he wasn't nearly finished yet. A high-noon showdown in the barracks hallway hadn't helped his friends outside, nor had it put them any closer to Pahlavi's sister—if, in fact, she could even be found inside the lab complex.

Bolan had no idea if she was alive or not, but he was bound to help Pahlavi try to find out. And that meant going through the soldiers who prevented them from reaching Building E. Rising, he moved off toward the far end of the hallway, checking each door closely as he passed, prepared for anything.

DARICE STUMBLED, nearly falling, as Gazsi pulled her along the corridor. She was barefoot, the concrete smooth and cold against her soles, with long cracks here and there where it had settled over time. No real attention had been paid to decorating storage space, unlike the other buildings in the complex, where a layer of vinyl flooring covered plain concrete.

Outside, she heard the fight still raging, automatic weapons hammering the night. Darice wondered how Gazsi planned to make it through that killing zone with just a pistol, but she reckoned he was counting on his rank to get him past the guards and through the gates.

Was there a chance that they would challenge him, perhaps even prevent him from departing with his prisoner? It seemed too much to hope for, and as that thought formed in her mind, she wondered why she should hope for it. Why wish to remain where men were killing one another, for whatever reason, when she had a chance to get away?

Because I won't, she thought.

That was the bottom line. With Gazsi, she would always be a prisoner, until he tired of her and put a bullet in her head, discarded her somewhere like so much trash along the highway. He would use her, lie to her, but he would never under any circumstances let her go.

Not now.

In which case, she decided, there was no point in cooperating with him any longer. If he meant to kill her one way or another, she could make him do it now, and maximize the bastard's inconvenience. If he thought she could assist him somehow in escaping from the compound, let him try without her.

Still, she had no stomach for a simple suicide. Darice decided it was best to wait until they were outside, then she'd break away from him and try to run. It didn't matter which direction, where she went. If nothing else, she could make Gazsi shoot her in the public eye, with witnesses, assuming all of them weren't so distracted by their efforts to remain alive that they entirely missed the show.

Perhaps someone would see, would file the memory away and bring it back to haunt Gazsi another time. Perhaps her sacrifice would not be all in vain.

Perhaps he'll miss!

The thought surprised her. She had never seen him shoot, had no idea if Gazsi was a practiced marksman or if carrying a gun was simply part of his persona, one more prop to make a small man seem larger than life. It might be that he couldn't hit a billboard with his pistol if he stood ten feet away. Perhaps he was inept, incompetent.

But if he missed, if she escaped—where would she go?

It was a problem she had not considered, and it struck her like a pail of cold water dashed into her face. They were five or six paces away from the exit, all manner of gunfire and shouting outside, plus the wail of a siren for background music, and Darice realized she had no plan at all.

She framed the compound's layout in her mind, the way she'd sketched it for her brother. She was in the maintenance and storage section—Building E—which meant the gates were located some three hundred yards to her left, as she stepped through the exit. If she ran in that direction, she would pass the motor pool and small garage that kept the plant's vehicles running, then a helipad they seldom used, and finally the western wing of Building A—thirty yards or so before she reached the gates.

It was a simple jog in daylight, with no one restraining her, without an army locked in battle all around. Given the circumstances as she found them, though, Darice supposed it might be the last thing she ever tried.

So be it, then, she decided.

At least she would have made the effort, without simply throwing up her hands in meek surrender.

At the exit, Gazsi clutched her wrist and used his knee to press the bar that would release the door, then shouldered through it, dragging her behind him. They had barely crossed the threshold into darkness speckled with flashes of gunfire, when the world in front of them went white and sizzling, nearly blinding her.

"Oh, God!" she whimpered, cringing, barely conscious of the fact that Gazsi had released her arm.

At first, Darice supposed it was the bomb exploding, but a heartbeat passed and she was not incinerated where she stood. Then she remembered that bomb was not completed, not assembled on the day of her arrest. Without some miracle that she could not envision, they would have had no working prototype so soon.

The lab was burning—melting almost seemed a better word—and shooting off white streamers that resembled something from a fireworks exhibition. Some kind of chemical explosion, she supposed, although Darice couldn't recall any materials in stock that would produce such an event. That only left munitions of some kind, presumably employed by those who were attacking the compound.

She said a silent prayer of thanks to whoever had destroyed Project X. She hoped the work was trashed beyond repair, the data lost beyond recall.

Gazsi was still aghast and gaping at the white-hot ruin of the laboratory when she struck him with her fist, putting her full weight behind it, giving it everything she had. He staggered, dropped to one knee, but she didn't wait to see him fall.

Before her heart beat twice, she was already off and running toward the distant gates.

DESPITE THE GUNFIRE in the hallway, Bolan caught the outside shooters by surprise. He counted five of them as he pushed through the exit, one just turning toward him with a questioning expression on his face, thrown off for just a second by the army uniform, then starting to recover as his eyes locked on the AKMS rising toward his face.

Bolan would never know if his first target registered the weapon, realized that it was wrong for anyone wearing his country's uniform. Maybe it was the threat alone that made the man backpedal, recoiling, with a warning cry to his companions building up a head of steam.

I'll warn them for you, Bolan thought, and shot the young man in the chest before he had a chance to speak. Three rounds ripped through his chest at something close to point-blank range, erupting from his back to spray and wound the nearest man behind him.

Bolan let the second wounded soldier curse and stagger for a moment, while he faced the other three. They panicked. One excited youngster squeezed off prematurely, knocking divots in the concrete wall beside him, fighting to control his weapon as its muzzle climbed.

Bolan fired from the hip, raking the three from left to right and back again, making them twitch and dance. His rifle wasn't made for close-range killing, but it did the job just fine, its small tumbling projectiles tearing massive wound channels through flesh and bone. There was no question of survival for the men on the receiving end. They dropped, already dead or dying, tremors from their final death throes mocking signs of life.

The man he'd wounded accidentally was trying hard to lift and aim his rifle with a broken arm. Given sufficient time, he might've managed, but the Executioner was in a hurry and he didn't want to die. A clean shot through the forehead dropped his final adversary like a puppet with its strings cut, plummeting into a lifeless heap.

Two of the dead had fallen where Darius could likely see them, but Bolan still used caution when he peeked around the corner, waving for his comrades to proceed. They ran to join him, bunching up like amateurs in the process, but Bolan didn't scold them once they were assembled under cover of the barracks building.

"What we need to do, right now—"

Pahlavi cut him off, pointing and crying out, "Darice! She's there!"

Turning, Bolan was just in time to see a woman in a white coat punch a man who held a pistol, swinging with all her might, as if she'd been collecting grievances for years and channeled all of them through her right arm. The man staggered and slumped, dropping to one knee, while the woman ran away. Bolan saw something awkward in her gait, as if she was unsteady on her feet—groggy, perhaps, or injured.

Darius ran after her before Bolan could stop him, calling out her name amid the gunfire and explosions. If she heard him, it would be a miracle. Then Bolan saw her stunned escort, raising his eyes and pistol, both of them locked onto Darius.

Cursing, Bolan rushed forward, fearing that he might already be too late.

23

Darius Pahlavi ran like one possessed, heedless of the danger to himself as bullets filled the smoky air around him. He cared nothing for the risk to himself, only for rescuing Darice and punishing—if possible—the people who had harmed her.

One of them was kneeling right in front of him. Pahlavi recognized Kurush Gazsi from one of those rare functions where Darice had pointed to him, whispering about his attitude and temper. It had been a kind of joke in those days, but Pahlavi saw no humor in the present situation.

Much less in the pistol Gazsi held, now pointed at himself.

Pahlavi started firing from the hip at twenty yards. He was not expert with the CETME rifle yet, though he had improved in the past few hours. Even so, his first few rounds fell short, chipping the concrete just in front of Gazsi, stinging him with fragments as they ricocheted. It was enough to spoil his target's aim, the first round out of Gazsi's pistol sizzling past him, on his left.

Pahlavi cursed the man who had done who knew what to his beloved sister, held her prisoner for days if nothing else, and this time when he fired, he brought the rifle to his shoulder. Not quite aiming, but directing it, the piece serving as an extension of his body and his rage.

The last rounds from Pahlavi's magazine ripped into Gazsi's

chest and throat, one drilling through his lower jaw and leaving it askew. The impact pitched his target over backward, sprawling with his legs folded beneath him in a position that would've caused agony to his knees if he was still alive.

Reloading on the run, Pahlavi saw his sister far ahead of him, approaching Building A. Her lab coat billowed for a moment as she ran, and he was shocked to see a glimpse of naked buttocks underneath. Why would she be—?

Seething, he turned back long enough to stamp on Gazsi's lifeless face and spit on the dead man before he ran on in pursuit.

"Darice!" he cried, straining his throat. "Darice, come back!"

She either didn't hear him, with the racket in the compound, or believed it had to be Gazsi chasing her. In any case, she ran as if a demon were behind her, breathing down her neck, making Pahlavi wonder if he had a prayer of catching her before she reached the gate and met more guards.

They might not shoot her down on sight, and yet—

As if his thoughts had been transformed to flesh, three soldiers chose that moment to emerge from Building A, directly in Darice's path. They saw her coming, hesitated in surprise—Pahlavi thought perhaps the coat had gapped in front, as well—and then moved out to intercept her.

Were they trying to be helpful?

That notion vanished as two of the soldiers grabbed Darice's arms. She struggled with them, kicking with bare feet until the third man gripped her ankles. Making faces, chattering among themselves, they started carrying Pahlavi's sister toward the door from which they had emerged short seconds earlier.

Pahlavi knew he could not let them go inside.

He stopped and aimed. Darice's life and his own depended

on his aim, how true it was, the steadiness of hand and eye. He chose the soldier on his left, aimed for the center of his broad, square back and squeezed the CETME's trigger almost lovingly.

Downrange, the soldier lurched, released Darice and toppled forward on his face. Before the others could react, Pahlavi had the second target in his sights, half turned in profile now, and fired another single round. It wasn't perfect, but it did the job, spinning the soldier on his heels and pitching him away, while Darice tumbled to the pavement.

Only one soldier remained, still clinging to her ankles, with the lab coat splayed and riding up around her waist. Still, sudden death detracted from the treasures on display. The soldier dropped her legs, reached for the rifle slung across his shoulder—and collapsed without a whimper as Pahlavi's bullet drilled him through the heart.

Pahlavi ran, then, calling to his sister as she clutched the coat around her, struggling to her feet. She heard him this time, turning, sobbing as she ran into his arms.

A moment later, she recoiled, arms tightly folded to prevent the coat from opening again. "You can't see me like this," she said. "It's—"

"Too late," Pahlavi said. "Come on. We're getting out of here."

"But, how?"

Turning, Pahlavi saw Bolan and the remnants of Ohm's fighting force approaching on the run.

"Trust me," he said.

IT WAS THE END of everything, and still Dr. Jamsheed Mehran was anxious to survive. His project, years of research, might be up in smoke, but he could always start again, set up another lab, collect another team. If only he could slip out of the compound without being killed or maimed, the rest would follow in its own good time, he was sure.

Huddled beside him in the shadow of the mess hall, watching men in uniform run back and forth across the compound, firing guns, Simrin Amira said, "I still don't understand. Why are the soldiers killing one another?"

"I don't know, and I don't care," Mehran replied. "If we stay here much longer, they'll be killing us. We have to reach the motor pool."

"Why not our own cars?" Amira asked.

"Use your head! They're twice as far away, up near the gate. We have to go in that direction, but I'd rather do it in a vehicle than try on foot."

"Well, then, what are we waiting for?"

Mehran could feel the angry color in his face. He didn't even want to think about his blood pressure. "Because *you* needed *rest!*" he snapped. "Have you forgotten that? It's only been a minute since you said—"

"All right!" she gritted at him. "I'm ready now. Can we just find a car and get away from here?"

Mehran peered to his left and right, saw no one close enough to trouble them on either side. Without another word, he rose and sprinted toward the motor pool, directly opposite their hiding place and forty yards away. It seemed like miles when he was running in the open, waiting for a bullet in the back to bring him down, but nothing happened and he reached the open shed in one piece, ducking between two plain sedans.

Amira tumbled in behind him, almost knocking him off balance until Mehran pushed her back. "Be careful there," she whined at him.

"Shut up and check for keys left in the cars," he ordered, rising as he spoke to peer in through the driver's window on his left.

The first car with a set of keys in the ignition was a Land Rover, but neither one of them could drive stick shift, and it was not the time to learn by trial and error. Three cars later, the next to last, they found keys in a black Peugeot sedan and Mehran slid behind the steering wheel.

He had the engine running when Amira started hammering the window on her side with frantic fists. Only the driver's door had been unlocked, apparently, and Mehran took another frantic moment learning how to open hers. When she was fuming in the seat beside him, Mehran backed out of the shed into the battleground and swung the wheel in the direction of the gate.

"Hang on," he said. "We can't afford to stop for anything."

"Just drive!" Amira said.

He accelerated toward the gate, watching combatants dive out of his way. It seemed to be instinctive, and he made no effort to decipher who was on which side. Indeed, as he'd informed Amira, Mehran had no clue why sides existed, or what all the fighting was about.

They'd covered nearly half the distance to the gate when someone fired a burst of automatic fire that strafed the car's right side. Mehran cringed from the ringing sounds of impact on the doors and fenders, flinched as glass imploded, and he nearly lost control when Amira squealed in pain.

"What is it?" he demanded, knowing what the answer had to be. She had either been cut by flying glass shards, or—

"I'm shot, you idiot!" she gasped.

Mehran hunched lower in his seat. If she was hit, it meant the slugs could find him, too. The vehicle could not protect them from incoming fire, but they might still escape if he drove fast and fearlessly.

"I'll get us out of here!" he said, speaking as much to his reflection in the rearview mirror as to the woman at his side.

Mehran floored the accelerator, barreling across the compound. He clipped one and then another soldier when they proved too slow in leaping from his path. Those impacts made him smile, unconsciously, a fierce grin totally devoid of warmth or humor. By the Peugeot's dashboard light, it made his face look like a leering skull.

"We're almost there!" he said, as they approached the bulk of the administration building. Just beyond it lay the gates and freedom, if he could negotiate—

Mehran was suddenly distracted by a group of people moving in the same direction, walking toward a clutch of military vehicles. They all wore army uniforms except for one, whose white lab coat stood out among the rest. Slowing to peer through the windshield, Mehran was stunned to recognize Darice Pahlavi.

Wasn't she supposed to be in custody? Where were the soldiers taking her? He wondered, feeling his panic rising.

As if she felt his gaze upon her, Darice turned to face Mehran. Their eyes met for an instant, then he noticed something strange about her lab coat. It was hanging open, and she seemed to be—

Darice pointed, said something to the soldiers, and they swung their guns around. Mehran took one hand off the wheel, waving at them and calling out for them to hold their fire. Beside him, Amira jerked upright, out of a daze, demanding, "What on earth—?"

The soldiers fired in unison, raking the car from end to end with automatic fire. Jamsheed Mehran shuddered as bullets ripped into his flesh, deaf now to Amira's screams. He kept his foot on the accelerator, but he could not seem to grip the wheel. He couldn't stop the car as it veered off and sped directly toward the nearest guard tower, was barely conscious of the shock as it collided with the tower's base.

Finished, he thought, and closed his eyes a beat before the crumbling tower buried him.

THEY PILED INTO THE STAFF car, Bolan in the driver's seat, two more beside him, while Pahlavi took the back seat, sandwiched between Janna and his sister. Bolan looked around for more of them and found two other Ohm members scrambling into the jeep—one at the wheel, one manning the machine gun.

Where were the rest? If any more were still alive, they hadn't made it back as planned.

"We're out of time," he told Pahlavi. "If we wait, we stay for good."

It was a leader's call. Pahlavi had to make it on his own. He craned his neck, then glanced at Janna and Darice. "The others must be lost," he said. "I saw most of them fall, myself."

Janna began reciting names, a doleful litany, but Bolan found it hard to follow. They'd come in with seventeen from Ohm, but Bolan couldn't wrap his mind around the dialect to count the names as she pronounced them.

"All dead, then," Pahlavi said a moment later. "We should go."

Bolan swung the staff car through a tight turn and saw the jeep do likewise in his wake. Behind them, scattered firing still peppered the compound, but he had to trust Pahlavi's judgment that the in-house troops were fighting one another now.

He hoped so, anyway.

How long before a panic call from someone involved in Project X brought reinforcements to the lab? Judging their distance from the nearest town or military base, he guessed they had another hour, give or take, by which time he hoped they would have ditched the military vehicles and uniforms, returning to civilian garb.

Returning to the house was a risk, but not as bad as starting fresh, stealing new vehicles and clothes. Once they were clear, Bolan would have one of Pahlavi's people man the staff car's radio and translate any bulletins suggesting that the house had been raided by their enemies.

Once they were clear.

A few soldiers were still clustered around the gate, and they began firing as Bolan's two-car caravan approached. Behind him, Bolan heard the heavy machine gun open up, its tracers streaking past the staff car, ripping into bodies by the gate.

The rebels in his car were firing, as well, one on each side from open windows as he steered them toward the gate. A bullet struck the staff car's windshield, right of center, punching through and burrowing between the seats. Bolan aimed his vehicle at the shooter, even as the gunman started taking hits, and plowed him under on their stampede toward the gate.

Another moment, and they blasted through it, running free and clear toward the highway with only scattered shots behind them and the heavy machine gun laying down a pyrotechnic screen of cover fire. Bolan continued for two miles at high speed, then backed off to a normal cruising pace and settled in for the long haul.

Their target was destroyed, most of the brains behind its operation liquidated. They had plucked Pahlavi's sister from the clutches of her captors, though recuperation was another matter, which doubtless would take some time.

It had cost them fourteen friendly lives.

How many dead men on the other side? Bolan had long since

given up on notching guns and keeping score. It hardly mattered, anyway, since predators were perfectly expendable. Kill one, and there would always be a dozen more to take his place.

The best the Executioner could do on any given day was thin the herd, and he had made a decent start on that in Pakistan. The rest was up to natives like Pahlavi and his sister, like the others who had risked their lives to step on Project X.

Tomorrow was their territory, and they'd have to handle it without the Bolan touch.

24

The airport terminal was crowded, as it had been on the day Bolan arrived. He had the feeling it was always crowded, people taking off and coming back as if they couldn't quite decide if it was worth the trouble to remain and see the story of their nation to its end.

Bolan, for his part, would be glad to get away.

He'd left Pahlavi and the others at the house, separated after saying their goodbyes and shaking hands around a circle that had shrunken perilously since their first meeting, less than twelve hours earlier. Pahlavi's sister needed care, and it would not be safe for Darius to show his face in public for some time. Bolan couldn't be sure that they had dealt with everyone who knew about Pahlavi's link to Ohm, for instance, and the same regime was still in charge as when they started, likely to desire revenge at some point in the not-too-distant future.

"You should leave," Bolan had told them all, Pahlavi translating. He'd watched the youngsters shake their heads, some of them smiling, others seeming on the verge of tears.

"This is our homeland," Pahlavi said. "We belong here. Where else should we go?"

"Someplace where you can live in peace until the wind shifts," Bolan answered. "I imagine you could find a place in the United States, if it came down to that."

"I am a Pakistani," Darius replied, "not Pakistani American. Your people do not want me. And, with all respect, I don't want them. We have a perfect right to live where we were born, raise children here, and live without a boot upon our necks or fear of being vaporized by warheads."

"Rights look good on paper," Bolan told him, "but they don't go far unless you've got the power to enforce them."

"We will have it yet, my friend. Come back and see us when that happens."

Bolan nodded, realized that he was talking to a stone. "Maybe I will," he answered, neither one of them believing it.

He'd driven to Lahore alone, ditching his surplus hardware on the way, a little at a time, until he only had his pistol and an extra magazine remaining when he reached the airport parking lot. He left them in a trash receptacle, ditched his rental car and checked in with a ticket agent for the airline that would carry him away in three short hours.

After that, it was a waiting game.

He watched soldiers as they patrolled the terminal in pairs, expecting them to question him, but none approached the tall man with his open magazine. He'd bought *Le Match*, although he couldn't read much French, on the off chance that seeing it would keep the soldiers off his back, and it appeared to work.

Or, maybe, none of them were hunting him at all.

He hadn't left a trail of any consequence in Pakistan, unless he counted the bodies scattered in his wake. His first encounter with the army had been accidental, and the second was in their effort to eliminate Pahlavi and his Ohm members, not to rub out an anonymous American. There was a possibility that soldiers or police would catch Pahlavi and his friends, would make them talk, but Bolan should be in the air by then, if not already safe in the U.S. They could describe him, blow the "Cooper" alias—and then, what?

Nothing.

He was clean, unless someone detained him at the airport for whatever reason, and he'd sanitized himself as much as possible before he'd reached the terminal. No weapons. Travel papers clean and very nearly genuine. No excess cash, no contraband, no souvenirs of any kind.

If anything, he might seem *too* clean, but the business cover would hold up if someone tried his contact numbers in the Untied States, all routed back to Stony Man Farm for automatic clearance in the case of an emergency. It might not stop some hotshot with a hard-on for Americans from holding Bolan past his scheduled departure time, but he'd done everything that could be done to head off such occurrences.

He started to relax with the announcement that his flight would soon be boarding. First-class passengers were summoned first. Bolan, whose seat was in an exit row around midfuselage, waited his turn to board while others disappeared inside the jet, then rose and followed them inside the belly of the beast.

The exit row had more leg room than usual, and Bolan had the window seat. He tuned out all the multilingual preparations for departure, already well-versed in fastening his seat belt and the other rituals that went along with takeoff. While the flight attendants spoke and displayed their skills, he watched the runway, half expecting military vehicles to swarm around the plane, but none appeared.

Ten minutes later they were airborne, westbound, leaving Pakistan and all her countless problems far behind. One of them was resolved for now, at least, but Bolan knew that it would only be a temporary fix. As long as men of varied creeds or races schemed to kill each other, there would always be another threat, and yet another after that, into infinity. Bolan supposed that it would take a fundamental change in human hearts and minds to make the world a truly safer place, and he had zero expertise in that regard.

As far as Bolan knew, he'd never changed a human heart.

He only stopped them cold.

Bolan allowed himself a glass of overpriced white wine with dinner from the galley's microwave. It wasn't great, but he was ravenous, needed the food before he went to sleep, hoping he wouldn't be disturbed before their next touchdown.

With any luck at all, he would not dream.

Epilogue

Arlington National Cemetery

Another walk among the tombstones, silently communing with the fallen. Some of them, he knew, had died civilians, years after their separation from the service, but they'd come from near and far to rest with comrades who had died in battle.

Coming home.

A few of the civilian dead were heroes in their own right—or, at least, renowned figures from history. John Kennedy was there, and Mississippi's Medgar Evers, murdered for his stand on civil rights five months before a sniper killed the nation's president in Dallas. Two of thousands who had touched their countrymen and maybe left the world a slightly better place.

Or not, depending on the watcher's point of view.

Bolan dismissed the vagaries of politics and waited for Hal Brognola to appear.

Footsteps sounded and Bolan turned to face his friend.

"You're always here ahead of me," Brognola said.

"I wouldn't want to keep you waiting."

"Nice tan," Brognola said.

"Comes with the territory," Bolan said.

"So, how'd it go?" the big Fed asked.

"I thought you'd probably tell me," Bolan replied. "I was a little close for an evaluation, but I think we did all right. Upset the applecart, at least."

"And burned the orchard too, from what I'm hearing on the air," Brognola said.

Bolan could only shrug. "There's nothing on television."

"Not *that* air. NSA's been monitoring traffic over Pakistan and India since you went in. We've got some saber-rattling on both sides right now, but not much worse than usual. The Indians are pretty sure something went wrong across the border, which improves their disposition all to hell, but they don't know exactly what it was or how close they came. Meanwhile, Karachi's going on about a flash fire at a fertilizer plant. No list of casualties available for who knows how long. Maybe never."

"No rebellion, then," Bolan said. "No warheads."

"Rebellion, in a paradise like Pakistan? You must be joking, son. As for the warheads, everybody knows they're sitting on a batch of nukes. Karachi won't admit they had a suitcase bomb fast-tracked to toast their neighbors, even if they don't mind leaking hints that it could happen any time," Brognola said.

"So, that's a nice fat slice of status quo," Bolan said.

"Pretty much the best that we could hope for in the circumstances."

"What about Ohm? Pahlavi and his sister and the rest?"

"Officially, of course, they don't exist. Denying or ignoring a rebellion means you can't be slapping rebels into jail. Bandits and public enemies are something else entirely, but they have to catch them first."

"So, no arrests?"

"As far as I can tell," Brognola said, "they're still at large. I won't say in the clear, because we know Pahlavi and his sister now have files that won't be closed until they're dead or sitting in a cage. As for whatever's left of Ohm, they're lying low, taking it one day at a time."

Bolan knew what that felt like.

"You're wishing there was more you could've done," Brognola said, trying to read his mind.

"There wasn't any more to do," Bolan replied. "Nothing."

"That's right. Remember that. You solved a problem. Made it go away, at least for now. No one expected you to change the world."

"It would be nice, though, wouldn't it?" Bolan asked.

"Maybe. Maybe not. Hell," Brognola said, "if the human race woke up tomorrow courteous and kind across the board, I wouldn't have a job. Neither would you."

"Would that be bad?"

Brognola shrugged. "It could be boring. How the hell do I know? Shit's been getting deeper every day since I was old enough to notice. It's the way things work. We grab a shovel and jump in. No way to stop it getting on you, but you always hope it doesn't get inside."

"Well, if it ever happens, you could always try philosophy," Bolan remarked.

Brognola's tone changed subtly as he asked, "You listen to the news this morning?"

"Pakistan's new missile? Right, I heard. They're saying they can drop a warhead in New Delhi if they're threatened. Makes you wonder, sometimes."

"If we should've skipped the whole damn thing?" Brognola asked.

"It just seems...I don't know."

"I think futile would be the word you're looking for," Hal said. "But I don't think it's accurate."

"I hope not," Bolan answered.

"I'm convinced it's not. You want a little more philosophy before we go have the world's greasiest burgers?"

"Let's hear it," Bolan said resignedly.

"Okay. I think we just do what we can, with what we have. Today, the Pakistanis claim they have a missile. Maybe it's true, and maybe it's not. Either way, they're on record about it. Doesn't mean some idiot won't use it, but at least the country's leaders will be on the hot seat to explain what happened, if it happens."

"Right. Okay."

"The deal you worked on was another thing, entirely," Brognola pressed on. "They would've used it. I've no doubt at all, and blamed it on the Sikhs or UFOs or whoever in hell they thought might take the rap. They would've done it just because they could, and just because they thought no one could prove they did it. And we stopped that. *You* did, rather. That's a good thing, I'd say. It's a positive. They can't sneak in and pull some crap without a ton of consequences falling on their necks. They'll think twice now, unless they're all stone crazy. And there's nothing anyone can do about it if they are."

Brognola had a point, Bolan realized. In fact, it was the only point of view that let him get up in the morning and continue with his lonely war. If Bolan started second-guessing every order, every move he'd made, he would be paralyzed with microscopic self-examination of his past until the pallbearers showed up to carry him away. His whole life, literally, might have been in vain.

And there was no way he believed that.

Not a chance in hell.

"I guess we wait and see about those missiles," he remarked.

"I guess we do. It's down to diplomats from this point, and you know how slow *they* move."

They started back toward the parking lot, leaving the ghosts behind. Bolan hoped they would rest in peace, but if they couldn't manage that, he hoped their restless dreams were not entirely grim. It was the best that he could wish them, after all their pain and sacrifice.

It was the best that he could wish himself.

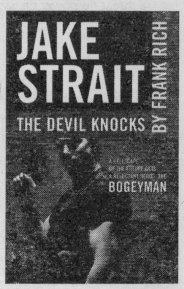

STARFIRE

Panic rocks the White House after an unknown killer
satellite fires a nuke into the Australian Outback—
a dire warning from an unknown enemy.
Stony Man is on the attack, racing to identify
the unknown enemy and using any means to
destroy it. As anarchy and mass murder push
the world to the edge, Stony Man hunts down
a threat no power on earth has yet faced....

STONY® MAN

*Available
April 2007
wherever
you buy books.*